Millie Marries a Marshal

Millie Marries a Marshal

Linda K. Hubalek

Butterfield Books Inc.

Lindsborg, Kansas

Millie Marries a Marshal: A Historical Western Romance
Brides with Grit Series: Book 2

Book ISBN-13: 978-1502828361

Library of Congress Control Number: 2014918686

Cover photo: This antique wedding photo is from the author's great grandparent's wedding album. There was no name or date on back of the photo.

Printed in the United States of America.

For an order blank for the Butterfield Books' series, please look in the back of this book, or log onto http://butterfieldbooks.com./

Retailers, Libraries and Schools: Books are available at discount rates through Butterfield Books Inc., or your book wholesaler.

To contact the author, or the publisher *Butterfield Books Inc.* please email to staff@butterfieldbooks.com or write to PO Box 407, Lindsborg, KS 67456.

Millie Marries a Marshal

Mail-order bride Millie Donovan was looking forward to meeting Sam Larson, a Kansas homesteader, who she is sure, from reading his heartfelt letters, will provide her with the love and safety she wants and needs. Millie arrives on the train, not realizing that her husband-to-be was killed in an accident, until Clear Creek's town marshal informs her of the situation.

Town Marshal Adam Wilerson never plans to marry due to his dangerous job. After reading letters found at his friend's home following his untimely death which were sent from his friend's mail-order bride, he can't help thinking of the woman, and believes he may be in love with her himself. But instead of sending Millie on the train back to her former home, he finds himself welcoming her—and her two-year-old charge—into his house, and into his heart.

When danger threatens, Millie faces it head–on to protect the people she loves, including the town marshal.

Can Adam keep the peace in town—and his house—or will the man following Millie cause an uproar that will endanger them both, and ruin their chance of a life together?

Books By Linda K. Hubalek

Butter in the Well Series

Butter in the Well

Prairie Bloomin'

Egg Gravy

Looking Back

Trail of Thread Series

Trail of Thread

Thimble of Soil

Stitch of Courage

Planting Dreams Series

Planting Dreams

Cultivating Hope

Harvesting Faith

Kansas Quilter Series

Tying the Knot

Patching Home (2015 release)

Piecing Memories (2015 release)

Brides with Grit Series

Rania Ropes a Rancher

Millie Marries a Marshal

Hilda Hogties a Horseman

DEDICATION

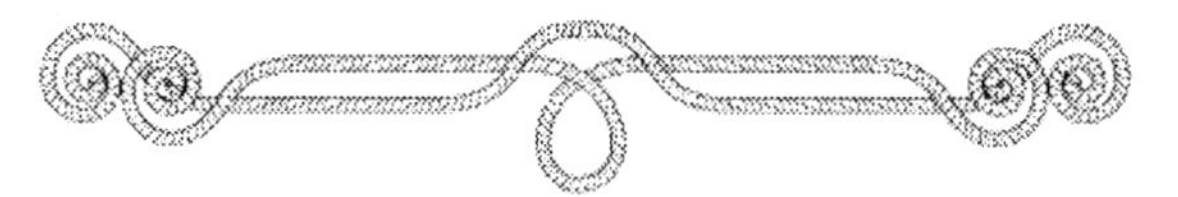

To women who have married lawmen, past and present—
Thank you for your badge of courage.

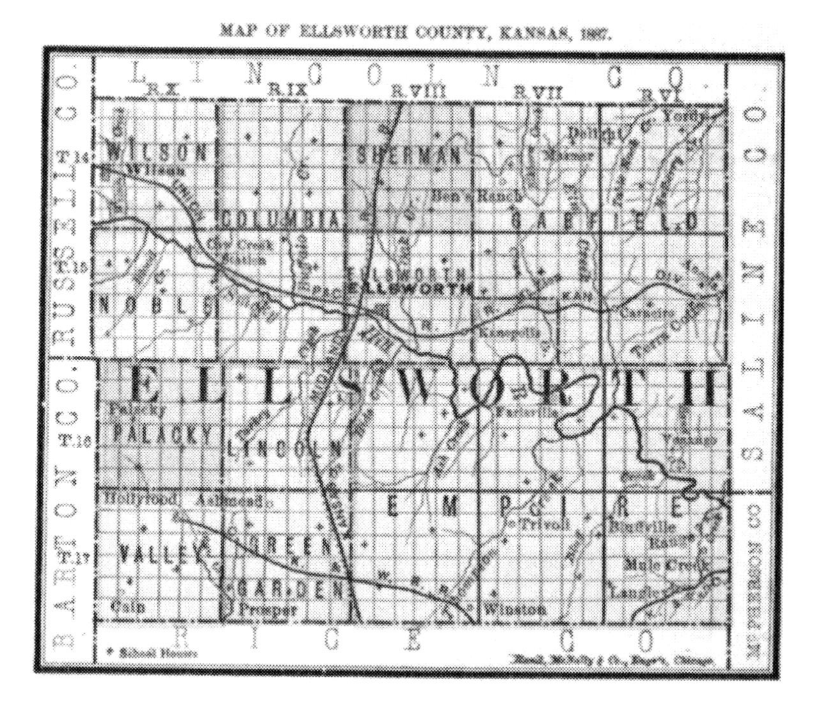

1887 map of Ellsworth County, Kansas.

CHAPTER 1

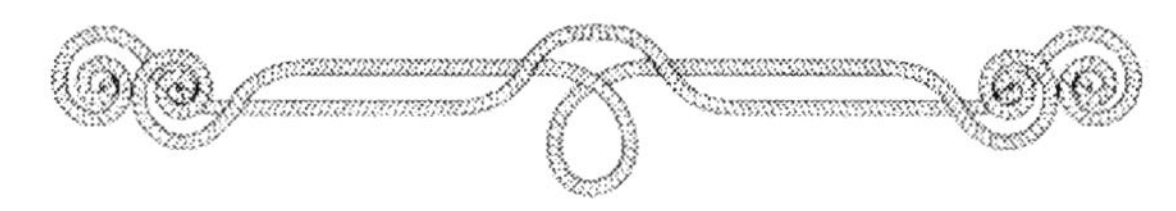

May 1872, Ellsworth, Kansas

Town marshal Adam Wilerson had been standing on the train platform for ten minutes and still didn't see a single lady who might be the woman he hoped to find. Adam's hazel eyes scanned up and down the boardwalk of the Main Street again, but didn't see any women he didn't know. Clear Creek was small enough that a stranger always stood out. Because of his job, he made it a habit to know everyone—and their business—in town.

Adam shifted through the four cardboard photographs of young women again. It was hard to compare a black and white photo with a real person, but he was accustomed to comparing wanted posters and criminal faces. None of these photos came close to featuring the few women who had arrived from any train this week.

He shifted the photos to one hand after another look down the boardwalk. Adam dug his watch out of his vest pocket, flicked the lid open to look at the time again. Finding it was only five minutes since the last time he checked; he closed and stuffed the watch back in his pocket.

Adam's mother was having a special early supper for his brother Jacob and fiancée Rania Hamner at the family ranch tonight, and Adam should have already been there. He pulled his wide-brimmed hat off his head to run his fingers through his light brown hair. It felt awfully short after visiting the barber today, but his ma insisted he get it cut before this Sunday's wedding. Out of habit, he smoothed his trim mustache with his right thumb and forefinger.

He'd met the train every day this week looking for a Miss Millie Donovan from Chicago, Illinois, but she had yet to arrive. He'd thought sure that she would be on today's train since it was Friday.

Adam wished he had some clue of who he was looking for, but could only guess because he really didn't have any idea what his former neighbor's fiancée looked like. After rancher Sam Larson died, the new occupants' daughter, Rania Hamner, when cleaning the house, found letters from a Miss Donovan who, obviously from the letters, was Sam's intended mail-order bride. Sam hadn't shared so much as a hint with Adam or his brother, Jacob, that he was writing to someone, let alone that he had proposed. Supposedly she was on the train this week and Adam had been meeting it every day, but no luck yet meeting the elusive woman. Her last letter said "you'll recognize me by my photograph" but there was no photo with the letters. Rania had earlier found four photographs when cleaning out a desk drawer but they weren't marked with any names, so Adam didn't know for certain whether this Millie Donovan was one of the four women pictured.

Adam sighed and looked around again. When Miss Donovan finally arrived he would have the unfortunate duty to deliver the sad news of Sam's death and help her arrange to return on the train to her former home. Because she and Sam hadn't married, this woman had no claim on his ranch or his belongings.

It was warm enough this May afternoon that Adam wished he could dispense with his own jacket and roll up his shirt sleeves, except it wouldn't look proper to greet the young lady he was supposed to meet.

His eyes kept returning to a crying little boy and his momma who stood a dozen feet away on the porch of the depot. She was having a time with the tired tyke who looked to be close to two years old by his walking, but he was so skinny it was hard to tell his age for certain. Adam didn't know them, but they had been waiting by the depot as long as he had. He saw them get off the train when it unloaded and appeared to be waiting for someone, too. Two worn carpetbags lay nearby with a little boy's coat lying on top of them. She hadn't claimed a trunk or any more bags from the railroad agent when he unloaded the train; must be visiting someone for just a day or two.

The kid was now wobbling circles around the mother, screaming like his shadow chased him. It was just the right pitch to make your eardrums bleed. With the tot's carrot–orange hair, there was no way the child could disappear in a crowd even if he was quiet. Adam chuckled when he thought how the boy was going to be teased when he became school-aged because of his bright hair. But that was his lot in life and he'd soon learn to stand up for his heritage of hair.

"Tate, *Tate*. Please stop and listen to me." The woman's distinct Irish lilt rose in frustration, drifting over to Adam. So far all he'd seen of the woman was the top of her little black hat, because she'd been looking down at the child the whole time. Her strawberry red hair, not quite as bright as the little boy's, but very curly, was tightly pinned up on the back of her head. It was a big knot of hair so he bet it was very long and wavy when she let it down at night.

Adam turned his back to the two, and nonchalantly stepped backward a couple of steps to hear this conversation better.

"Dada was …" The train whistle blew announcing its pending departure so Adam didn't hear what else the boy cried as he shrunk against his mother.

The woman crouched down and held the boy to her side. "No, Tate. Please listen to me. Mr. Larson will be a good man. He's not like…"

The train whistle blew again as she was continuing her conversation with the boy, cutting off Adam's hearing the conversation again.

Adam whirled around when he heard the lady mention Mr. Larson. He had read the stack of letters that Sam had received from the woman, and there was no mention that she was a widow, let alone had a son.

Adam took off his hat and held it on his chest before taking two steps forward and asking, "Miss Millie Donovan?"

The woman's green eyes turned up to meet his hazel ones to acknowledge his presence. She stood up straight and pasted a smile on her face, probably thinking she was meeting her intended. "Mr. Larson?"

"NO, NO!" The little boy screamed at the top of his lungs while rushing forward to pummel Adam's knees with his tiny fists.

***

Millie froze when Tate attacked the legs of the tall man. He bent his wide shoulders down to clamp his hands on the unruly child and attempt to peel him off his legs. He had dropped his wide-brimmed hat in Tate's mini attack, and Millie got a good look at his neatly trimmed light brown hair. The man wasn't at all like Millie had pictured Sam to be, but it gave her heart a flutter to find out he was so tall and handsome.

Now Tate—with tears trickling down his cheeks and his thumb in his pouty mouth—was being settled on the man's hip and he turned his attention to her again. "Miss Donovan?"

"Yes," Millie breathed, relieved to finally meet her husband.

"Miss Donovan, I'm sorry to…"

"Star!" Tate screamed, interrupting the man as he punched the marshal badge on the front of the man's shirt.

Millie stared at the object then up at the man's face. His face twitched as he gave her a look that said he wasn't amused by the boy's second attack on his person.

He thrust the tot at arm's length, but Millie stared at the badge instead of taking Tate. *Oh Lord, have we run into more trouble than we ran away from? Sam never mentioned in his letters that he was the town marshal besides a rancher.*

"Miss Donovan?" Millie realized the lawman wanted her to take Tate, so she took the boy and hugged him to her shaking chest. "Ma'am, could we walk over to my office so we can talk?"

"My bags …"

"Your bags will be fine here with the depot agent for a minute. Please come with me."

Millie followed behind the determined man as he strolled down the dusty boardwalk in front of them. He reached the marshal's office several seconds before she did because of his clipped pace, and already had the door open and waiting for her to walk in.

"Please have a seat, and hold on to your boy so he doesn't get into anything he shouldn't."

That remark made Millie's spine stiffen and her red-haired courage flare. Sam mentioned he loved children, so Millie couldn't believe his callous demeanor towards Tate. She gripped Tate around his waist and firmly set his little bottom on her lap as she sank into the wooden chair in front of the marshal's desk. The lawman continued to stand behind the desk until she had Tate under control—for a few seconds.

"Miss Donovan, I'm Marshal Adam Wilerson, and I regret to tell you that Sam Larson is dead."

When the marshal's blunt words sunk in, Millie felt Tate's body slide out of her arms as the room blacked out of her sight.

***

Now what? Adam kneeled beside the woman on the floor as the crying boy ran circles around his desk. This is not how his usual day went. Adam would prefer the swinging fists of any drunken cowboy over this distressed mother and her uncontrollable child.

Just as Adam dipped his handkerchief in the water pail that sat on the nearby table, she slowly came to. Although, by now, Adam would have preferred to wipe the wet cloth across his own face, he handed it to Miss Donovan. She patted her face, then grabbed the boy to scrub his tear-streaked face, asked the little boy to "blow" his nose—and then handed the snot-filled cloth back to him.

Adam stayed silent as the woman gathered her composure—and the wayward child—back in the seat in front of his desk. At least now the tot was subdued with his thumb stuck in his mouth, and baby drool running down his chin, again.

"Miss Donovan…or should I be calling you Widow Donovan?" He paused a second, because she wasn't wearing all black like a widowed woman, but she just nodded her head and didn't say which name he should use. "I'm sorry to inform you that Sam died in a riding accident. Your letters were among his things, but I didn't have a way to contact you. Your last letter said you were stopping at your sister's a while, but her name and address weren't mentioned."

Adam continued because she didn't say anything. "Because you and Sam weren't married yet, I'm afraid there isn't anything I can give you except advice. It would be best if you get back on the train and travel back to Illinois or to your sister's family."

"No! Um…no…my sister…is…no longer there."

That information stunned Adam. She just lost her sister and then he had to give her this news? *My word, no wonder she collapsed.* Adam cleared his throat and spoke with compassion this time. "I'm sorry for your loss. Could your sister's husband help you?" This time the woman didn't meet his eyes when she shook her head no, but he noticed she tightened her hold on the boy. "Do you have somewhere else you could go?"

She rubbed her forehead as if trying to erase the bad news she just received. Then she looked up, not into his eyes but at his badge. "I'll have to think about this," she replied in a weary voice.

Adam extended his hand to the woman, waiting for her to rise out of the chair, trying to get her out of his office so he could head out to the ranch. He didn't know what else to do for this poor woman and upset child. "I'll collect your bags and walk you over to the hotel, Miss Donovan."

***

Millie was afraid she'd faint again before the marshal got out of sight. She was so relieved when she first saw him, or who she thought was Sam Larson. She thought her luck had turned around when she saw his strong stature and clear, kind eyes. She and Tate would be okay here—in the middle of nowhere—also known as Clear Creek, Kansas.

She let out a slow breath, trying not to hyperventilate. The news of Sam's demise was devastating to her plans, but having a lawman know where she was…made things worse.

Marshal Wilerson was more than ready to deposit her bags inside the hotel's door and removed himself just as quickly, not even waiting to catch the hotel clerk's eye to indicate that Millie needed assistance. He mumbled something about a family dinner he was late for and excused himself.

Millie had let him go, because she needed to get away from him, too. After looking out the hotel door to be sure he was out of sight, Millie scooted the bags out the door while wrangling Tate.

"Ma'am, may I help you?" The clerk had been busy with a guest when they first arrived, and was now ready to assist Millie.

"No, thank you," Millie said as she slammed the door practically in his face.

Now what? "Tate, you're going to have to walk while I get these bags." Millie grasped the bags and coat, looking up and down the Main Street of this little town. Sam had sent her money for the train ticket so she had the fare to get here. Unfortunately, she had no extra money along because she had stuffed it into her sister's hand before picking up Tate and running to the train station.

Millie took stock of Tate's appearance, due to the smell that reeked from his pants. She didn't have time to grab many of Tate's things when they left in a hurry, so Tate only had a few diapers along. How was she going to wash and dry his little items? A bath would do wonders for both of their spirits too, but that was unlikely to happen anytime soon.

She sighed, turning her face up to the sky to mutter, *"Now what, Da?"* She never thought she'd be living on the streets again like she did in her old Conely's Patch neighborhood after the Great Chicago fire two years ago, but that's what it seemed would be her fate. Well, it was going to be "beg, borrow or steal" if she and Tate were going to eat and sleep tonight. She had lived through it before and would again, only then she didn't have a toddler to worry about.

CHAPTER 2

"I told you Ma, there was nothing I could do. When Miss or maybe I should say when 'Widow' Donovan arrived—with this little orange-headed brat in tow—I told her about Sam, and then escorted her to the hotel. I did my duty, end of story."

This was not the reception he expected when arriving at his brother's ranch this evening. The Wilersons, Hamners, and some friends were all here celebrating Jacob and Rania's engagement. As a surprise for his Swedish immigrant bride, Jacob had painted the washhouse a dark "Falun Red" and planted flowers around the little building to remind Rania of her childhood home in Sweden. Picnic tables were set up outside by the backyard "Swedish scene" and everyone was seated, enjoying a bountiful food spread when he arrived.

Adam was ready to sit down and fill his own plate, but that changed in an instant when he told his mother why he was late. His ma was at his side with her finger pointed up in the air at his nose in a second.

Four women stared at him, like he was a dunce that should be standing with his nose in the corner of the old school house.

"How could you be so rude and crude, Adam? I raised you better than that," his mother, Cate, asked in exasperation. It had been a long time since she'd ask that question. Probably then she looked *down* at him, not up. It didn't help that his sister, Sarah, and the blonde Hamner twins, Rania and Hilda—at least still seated—all had their arms crossed in unison disgust at him too. His brother Jacob sat smirking and probably thinking, *you're in deep manure now, Brother.*

Adam thought they'd be glad that the woman had finally arrived, and been told of Sam's demise so she could get on with her life.

Instead, the women asked him umpteen questions that he never thought to ask Miss Donovan. Where did she come from and what was she going to do now? Why didn't they know she had been married before and had a son? Why didn't he take them to the café to eat a meal before checking them into the hotel? And there was room in the hotel, right, even with all the cattlemen coming into the area with the cattle drives?

That last questions did make him a little uneasy because he wasn't positive she got a room. The whole family had read the letters that Millie Donovan had written to Sam, so the women felt invested in the drama. Apparently they were wishing they could have met the lady themselves, because they asked—in detail—what Millie looked like.

"So which picture was she, Adam?" Hilda, Rania's outspoken twin was asking about the four photographs they had all studied, but he never looked at the photographs again after hearing Miss Donovan say "Mr. Larson."

"Don't know, Hilda. I didn't stop and compare each one next to her face." Adam picked up a chicken leg from his plate and attacked it to fill his mouth with something to chew on besides his blasted conscience.

Adam thought of Millie's red hair, a few tight curls hanging loose from her tight bun. Her green Basque shirtwaist and black skirt weren't very clean, but after traveling on a dirty train with that crying boy—it's a wonder she didn't look worse. He did feel sorry for her having to handle the child alone, though. Maybe the boy was sick. He was so thin and he cried the whole time Adam saw him, well, except when he spied his marshal's star. Then the kid had a screaming meltdown.

Where did she come from? He had no idea if she had been on the train for a day or a week. *What kind of marshal was he*? It was his job to know what was going on in town and that young woman and child had just fogged up his brain. *Why?*

Ethan Paulson, Sarah's fiancé, leaned forward and added to the conversation, "I'm sure the Simpson Hotel is full, because we've had constant visitors asking when our new hotel will be open. As soon as we have the open house and wedding, it will be full to capacity."

Adam glanced over at Sarah, who had stopped glaring at him to look down at her plate. The Paulson family was near to completion with their new hotel, and planned for Ethan and Sarah to manage it, while living there. Their wedding was to be the hotel's open house event. Ethan was a good man, handsome with his slicked back blonde hair, but more than a decade older than Sarah. The spark of wedding excitement wasn't in Sarah's eyes like they were in Rania's. Adam hated for Sarah to settle for a loveless marriage, but his mother insisted that it was her call and the brothers were to stay out of it.

“Is there somewhere else she can stay?” Rania inquired. “I suppose the boarding houses are full too.”

“I heard the two houses in town are full with permanent boarders at the moment,” answered Ethan, since he had the inside track on the lodging in town.

His mother finally sat back down. “Please check to be sure they are in the hotel tonight, Adam. You owe that to Sam, and *you be sure* they get on the train tomorrow too. Will she travel back to her sister’s?”

“Ah. I don’t think so. Her sister died while she was there.” Adam cringed and squeezed his eyes shut, because he knew his mother was going to really be steamed when he revealed that tidbit.

"Adam Moses Wilerson….”

Adam had already decided he would confirm with the hotel manager that Miss Donovan was settled into a room when he got back tonight. He always made rounds about ten o’clock to check the businesses, streets and alleys, so it wouldn’t be any extra work to be sure they were all right.

“I’ll be sure she’s all right, Ma. I assume she’ll go back on the east train…to somewhere…tomorrow, so it will be 12:15 p.m.”

The four women glanced at each other, each signaling the other with a raised eyebrow. Adam guessed one—or all of them—would be in town checking on Sam’s mail-order bride before it was time to partake of forenoon coffee.

***

Lucas Boyle stood in the open doorway of his livery stable with his arms crossed and his legs in a wide stance when Adam rode Cannon, his silver dapple dun horse, into the low light shining from a kerosene lamp hanging just inside the door.

“Who put the burr under your saddle, Boyle?” Adam questioned the man as he swung out of Cannon’s saddle.

“I just caught that little red-headed lady and her screaming tot in the hayloft again. That’s the second time I sent them on their way. I feel sorry for them, but the kid’s so noisy it’s scaring the horses in the stalls below them. Don’t know where she ended up after they left the livery, but I hope she found somewhere to get that little kid off the streets.”

“I met them by the depot earlier today. She was supposed to be Sam Larson’s mail-order bride,” Adam sighed.

“Well, why didn’t you take care of them? You’re the marshal,” Boyle asked accusingly.

Adam looked down, digging the heel of his boot in the dirt and grinding it back and forth, just like his back teeth were doing at the same time. “She said she’d take care of herself, and I delivered her to the door of the hotel before I left for Jacob’s ranch this afternoon.”

“You know that place was full, Marshal. Clancy said he caught her rummaging through the trash in the alley behind his café, too. Probably looking for food besides shelter.”

Adam tilted his head back and sighed. *Lord, help me if my mother finds out that fact.* “Which way did they go? I’ll go look for them after I take care of Cannon.”

“I’ll take care of your horse tonight, you see after that mother and her baby.”

"Yes, Sir," Adam muttered. Now he had another concerned parent stewing after the two wandering strangers.

Adam hunted up and down Main Street, the alleys behind all the businesses and every other place he could think of—before finding them—*no, hearing them*—in an abandoned chicken house. He had just given up, walked in the back door to his own little house behind the jailhouse, and then heard whimpering—from the tiny shack in his own backyard.

He went into the kitchen, to light a lantern before venturing into the dark backyard. After a second thought, he pulled his revolver before opening up the chicken house door and swinging the lantern into the doorway. A second later he peeked around the corner, not wanting his chest blown to bits in case he was wrong and it was a thief, or drunk with a gun.

Miss Donovan was crouched in the corner, shielding the boy with her body, with one hand up to keep the bright lantern light from shining in her eyes.

"Miss Donovan, would you please come out of my chicken house?"

"Marshal Wilerson?"

"Yes. Please come out."

"No. Tate needs some shelter tonight and this seems to be it in town," she wearily answered Adam.

"You can spend the night in the jail. It's unoccupied at the moment." Holding the lantern high to shine the way, Adam saw Miss Donovan struggle with the boy and two bags again. "I'll get the bags. You carry the boy to the jail."

Adam watched Miss Donovan stand stiffly before hitching the whimpering boy higher up on her hip. The kid was swaddled in a ladies' dress and the woman didn't have on a coat. Adam realized that Miss Donovan wasn't in much better shape than the boy when he took a good look at her hollow cheeks and the dark rings beneath her eyes. Adam felt bad, realizing the spring night had turned chilly and the pair didn't have proper outer garments.

"Did you eat supper tonight?" Silence met his question. "Miss Donovan?"

She sighed and Adam had to lean close to her to hear say, "No, sir."

"Don't you have any money?"

"No, I used up my funds getting here."

"I'm sorry to have added to your trouble by not helping you this afternoon. Let's get into the jail where you can both lay down. It's late, but the saloon's kitchen should have sandwich fixings and maybe some milk for the boy, so I'll fetch something for you to eat."

***

Adam walked back into his house an hour later after getting the Donovans settled in the jail cell bunk. Because it was time for his late evening rounds, he did that on his way to the saloon. The barkeeper waved him to the back where he found supplies to make a couple of bread and butter sandwiches. There wasn't any milk left from the evening so he'd be sure to bring some to the boy in the morning. The two ate the sandwiches, drank some water and promptly fell asleep as he watched over them.

He felt badly after seeing the mother and son devour those simple sandwiches. When was their last meal?

What was he going to do with them tomorrow? Adam's mind kept pulling up the image of the little lady and her tot, causing him to stay awake for a long while.

CHAPTER 3

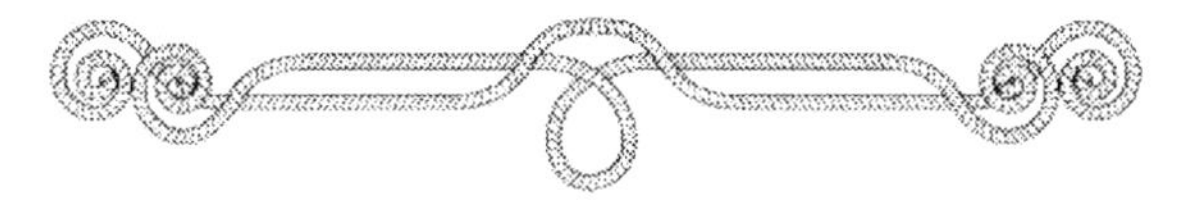

"I'm already in jail? Millie froze, looking at the cell bars just a few feet from the smelly cot where she lay. But the door wasn't shut on the cell. And movement against her chest caused her to jerk with relief. Tate was still under the blanket that covered her shoulders, snuggled up against her, using her body heat. Millie realized not all the smell was coming from the cot's covering. The poor child must be past exhausted because he'd be raising a fit about his dirty diaper if he felt up to it.

Millie closed her eyes, trying to determine what her options were. *There are always options, Lassie, even if it's down to fight or flight.* How many times had she heard her father say that over the years? It was his mantra to keep pushing her and her sister, Darcie, through all the adversity and tragedy they had to face.

Her parents Ennis and Morna Donavon, along with her brothers Flynn and Galen, chose to flee Ireland during the Great Potato Famine, finally settling in the Irish area called Conley's Patch in Chicago. After losing two infant sons at birth, Morna gave birth to her sister Darcie, and then Millie.

Ennis fought for jobs—literally with boxing matches—to take care of his family, finally obtaining the role of a policeman. It was a dangerous job, but the six of them had food and shelter, and life was better than what they left in Ireland—so her parents said. Then the Civil War hit when Millie was ten years old. By the time it was over, her brothers had died in eastern battles and their mother from consumption.

There are always options…until the Great Chicago fire burned their home leaving the three of them homeless. Her father disappeared into the job of helping others, Darcie married Curtis Robbins, and Millie moved into a room above the bakery where she found a job.

Millie's middle growled, deepening the hunger pangs that had been gnawing in her stomach since leaving her sister's home in St. Louis four days ago. Neither of them had a good full meal since then, only finding leftovers half-wrapped in trash cans along the way. So her option today was to fight—to find food, shelter and a job—while hiding from the law.

And here I sit in jail…

***

"Nonsense Adam, she can stay at your home for a few days until Millie decides what to do. You can bunk in the jail."

"Ma, my house isn't…uh…clean…"

Millie listened with hope as the marshal's mother told her six-foot son what *his* solution to Millie's predicament should be. And although he tried to give excuses, Millie was impressed that the man respected his mother and her decisive statement. Millie carefully sat up on the edge of the cot, not wanting to waken Tate. She looked out to see the marshal and two women standing by his desk. The trim woman with matching brown hair to her son's must have been young when she married, because she looked like she could be an older sister to Adam instead of his mother. The younger woman, about her own age, must be a daughter, and the marshal's sister, although she had darker hair.

Marshal Wilerson had brought them a heaping plate of biscuits and gravy, and a pint bottle of milk from the café the first thing this morning. It was the perfect soft meal for Tate to eat and fill her starving stomach too. After cleaning up the two of them the best she could in the basin of water the marshal had brought in to her, she laid Tate back on the cot, and apparently fell back to sleep herself until the conversation in the other room awakened her.

"Mother," the younger woman touched her mother's arm and nodded toward Millie. "She's awake now."

Millie rose and rubbed her hands down her skirt as she acknowledged the women coming toward the cell. Here came possible help, so Millie stepped out the door and extended her hand with, "Hello, nice to meet you, Mrs. Wilerson."

"Millie, please call me Cate, and this is my daughter, Sarah." Cate grasped Millie's hand and pulled her into a full embrace. "We were so sorry to hear of your sister's death, and then to find out about Sam too." Cate glanced around Millie to chance a look at the little boy still asleep in the pile of blankets. "Looks like your son's content for a bit, so let's go into the office to talk."

What? Her sister was dead? Millie's mind searched for conversations she had with the marshal, trying to figure out how he got that idea. Or could it really be true? Had he gotten a wire from St. Louis this morning? *No.* Only Darcie knew where Millie was, so the marshal had assumed wrong. Maybe it would help her, and Darcie's plan, for others to believe that until they could move on. Sam dying had ruined their plans.

The marshal pulled his chair around next to the one in front of the desk and motioned for the women to use them. The marshal and Sarah stood back while Cate sat down in one wooden chair and pulled Millie down in the other.

"Adam said you don't plan to travel back home, so what do you want to do now?"

"Well, I have no choice but to find lodging and employment here. I'll get my bearings and start looking for both after Tate catches up on his sleep. The…events and travel have been very hard on him."

"It looks like it's been hard on you too, dear." Millie sensed Cate looking her over with concern, taking in her dirty clothing and pale face. "Sam was a great neighbor to us, and he would have made a fine husband and father. The Wilerson family will help you anyway we can."

Millie breathed a sigh of relief that she might have found a kind soul in this woman, and her family, seeing Sarah nodding a smile in encouragement.

"Adam and I were just discussing…" Cate paused and looked at her son, "that you will stay in his house while you get your bearings." Millie saw the marshal take a deep breath before agreeing with a reluctant nod.

"Millie, you've spent days on the train grieving, plus trying to keep your little boy occupied. You must be exhausted and tired. Then to be given the news that Adam gave you? And I'm sure in a very blunt way." Cate looked up at her son again. "I think you would have collapsed at the news." Millie didn't want to tell Cate that was what had happened right here in her son's office yesterday.

Millie looked at Adam, who just put his hands up in the air in surrender to his mother. "Are you sure there isn't any other place for us to stay? I hate to put the marshal out of his own house."

"If you can't travel back home, you need to find a job, or another husband." Cate paused and tilted her head as if in thought. "Adam eats all his meals at the café—or the saloon—and has someone wash his clothes too. And his house is always a dusty mess as you'll soon see." Now Cate's smile turned downright mischievous. "I think he'd be ahead to have a live-in housekeeper who could fix meals and in general, take care of him. How would you like the job—at least for a while—in exchange for room and board?"

***

Adam pounded down the boardwalk, making the boards rattle with every measured boot step. He was supposed to be keeping the peace in town instead of picking up a woman's bags and bringing them to *his* house. What the heck was his mother up to? He was almost scared to leave the three women alone while he went home to hastily clean the worst off the floor in his bedroom, and living room, and... *Oh heck*, Adam shuddered with a thought. Maybe his mother was playing matchmaker for him.

He knew that his mother had given advice to his brother Jacob about Rania Hamner, one of the daughters of the Swedish immigrants who had bought Sam Larson's place. Jacob went over to the Hamner place *every day* at his mother's insistence, to check on Rania—and her dog and two sheep—while her parents traveled back on their last trail drive from Texas to Ellsworth before permanently settling in Kansas. He wasn't surprised when Jacob proposed to Rania.

Then there was his mother's urging to let Rania's twin, Hilda, buy his brother Noah's homestead. Noah had traveled to Illinois to bring back Victoria, his intended bride—but when he arrived, he found she had already married someone else. Noah had yet to come home months later, and a claim jumper almost took over his place before his mother and Jacob decided to sell it to someone they knew. Adam knew his ma was hoping for a second match between the two families—whenever Noah decided to come home.

His mother had even helped Dagmar Hamner, Rania and Hilda's brother, adjust to his new home on the Bar E Ranch. It was a good thing, because the owner's daughter from Boston recently arrived, throwing Dagmar into a panicking tailspin. If his mother hadn't had to deal with Rania's kidnapping, and then her and Jacob's wedding to plan this last week, she would have run to help Dagmar greet Cora Elison as soon as she learned that the young woman had set her dainty foot inside the front door of the house on the Bar E.

Ma was leaving his sister Sarah alone though. Although everyone liked Ethan and his parents, all of the Wilersons secretly thought Ethan wasn't the perfect match for Sarah. They acted like brother and sister instead of future bride and groom, but Cate insisted her three sons were not to interfere with their sister's choice of husband.

Adam's parents had a wonderful partnership until his father, Moses, died four years ago of cancer. Adam didn't think he could ever find a woman to match his parents' love, so he had decided to stay a confirmed bachelor, especially with his dangerous career. Adam didn't want his mother interfering with his choice of life, but he had a feeling she was already meddling.

***

Thanks be to Saint Catherine! Millie's Roman Catholic upbringing came to mind when she stood in front of Adam's home. She didn't get a good look at this particular house last night when they sneaked into the abandoned chicken house. Now the sight of the small, two-story home was like a beacon of light to Millie's weary soul.

The clapboard house was painted white, and the porch floor a light gray. Compared to some of the unpainted shacks in town she'd seen from their "alley walk" last night, this was a nice home. The porch had a porch swing and two other chairs on it, and Millie could imagine complementing the space with a big pot of red geraniums.

Not that she'd ever owned a pot of flowers in her life, or lived in this nice of house, but she'd seen both in Chicago—in better neighborhoods than where she lived. Her family had resided in tenant housing until the fire wiped out those blocks of shoddily-built living quarters.

The room she lived in above the bakery was small, hot in the summer and freezing in the winter, with slanted ceilings so there was only the middle area to stand up straight. The marshal's house looked like a mansion at the moment.

Cate waltzed up the porch steps and opened the door to her son's home. "Please come in, Millie. I know my son isn't the best housekeeper but you'll find it a good place to rest and get your bearings."

Millie took a step into the home, and then stopped in awe. Sunshine filtered in through the large windows—along with dust motes—but the space was inviting and homey, even if a few newspapers and a pair of socks were on the dining room table. She could write her name in the dust that covered the surfaces of the nice furniture, but a simple dusting would take care of that.

They entered into a combination of living and dining room, with the parlor to the right. Comfortable furniture filled both rooms. A mantel clock resting on a wall shelf in the living room gave a soothing tick-tock to the otherwise quiet room. Millie could just imagine Adam sitting in the rocker at the end of the day with his stocking feet on the upholstered ottoman.

Millie followed Cate through the first room to the kitchen behind, and then right into a small bedroom off of it. Millie was as wide-eyed as Tate was while they followed Cate and Sarah around the house.

"Adam uses one of the bedrooms upstairs, so this room will be perfect for you and Tate."

Cate pulled open the shade on the only window in the room, unlatched the lock and tugged open the window. "Let's get some fresh air in here while I show you around."

The room had a single bed, wash stand with a pitcher and basin sitting on its top, a wooden rocker and a small chest of drawers. And the colorful quilt on the bed made the room delightful.

Millie couldn't believe the luck of the Irish was with her in Kansas!

"Adam, please bring their bags in here, then walk over to Pastor Reagan's house and see if you can borrow their high chair. I think their last boy is large enough to sit in a regular chair by now."

Next, Cate looked around the kitchen. "Now about food... Adam, do you have anything in your pantry besides cobwebs?"

Sarah looked in kitchen drawers until she found a pencil and paper and sat down at the kitchen table, ready to right down what her mother said they'd need.

"Ma, there's no need to buy groceries since I'm never home for meals," Jacob warned.

Cate stuck her head back out of the walk-in pantry and stared at her son like he had no sense at all. "Adam. You have guests in your home and the hospitable thing to do is feed them while they are here." Sarah snickered in her hand while the two faced off.

"Fine, buy a few groceries, but I'm not cooking the meals." He turned to Millie. "Can you cook a decent meal?" Cate huffed at Adam's question but Millie was prepared to answer.

"Actually, I cooked and baked in an upscale restaurant in Chicago, so I think you will find my meals better than any café in this one-horse town." She stared at Adam, daring him to cut her down. She might have stretched the truth a bit about how fancy the restaurant was where she worked, but if he kept up with his attitude, his face would be wearing the first flaky-crust pie she'd bake.

"Fine. I'll look forward to first-class uppity meals then," he muttered as he sauntered out the back door.

"Sarah, I think we'll buy the basics and whatever Millie wants to make, because there is nothing worth eating in the pantry."

Millie was thinking about the other things she needed for Tate too. "How about milk for Tate?" She hated to bring it up, but she had no funds of her own for Tate's needs.

"There's a farmer on the edge of town who brings in milk to the mercantile each day. I'll be sure to order milk for you to pick up each morning."

Cate looked again at Tate. "How about diapers? Does he have a good supply? And we need laundry soap…I doubt Adam has any in the house."

"I'm afraid I brought along a limited supply of diapers, because I had to carry our bags plus him." It wasn't the total truth, but it was hard to keep track of Tate and two bags. "I couldn't wash on the train so I need to wash all his diapers and clothing today if possible."

"We'll buy diapers so you'll have extra."

Sarah looked out the kitchen window into the backyard then turned and asked, "Does Adam have a clothes line or clothes pins?" Millie was mentally tallying up the cost of everything they mentioned and getting dizzy thinking about it. She expected to move in with Sam, and all those things would have been in place in his home. How was she going to repay Cate or Adam for their supplies and hospitality?

"Cate, this is too generous of you. I can't pay you back…"

"Millie, I'm going to charge it to Adam's account, not mine," she smiled broadly. "Because you can cook, and I assume wash clothes, he's going to be money ahead to have you take care of him in exchange for room and board."

CHAPTER 4

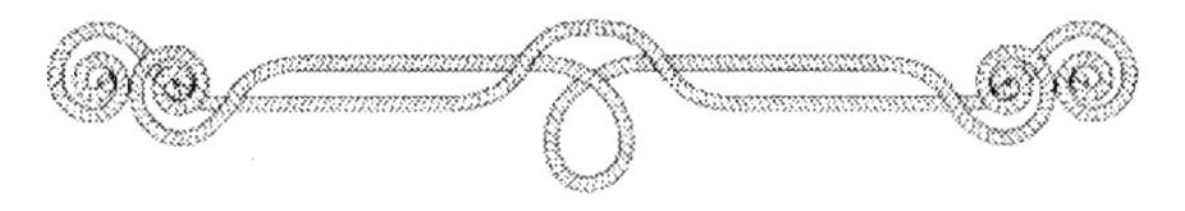

Jacob Adam couldn't *believe* he was walking back from the Reagans, holding a high chair slung over his back with one hand and cradling a baby potty chair against his chest with the other. It was only a three-block walk from the pastor's house to his, but he'd found more people on the street watching him pass like he was a parade. *Dang that woman and her child. No, dang it for Sam dying and leaving him to take care of his new family.*

Mrs. Reagan could have filled a wagon with all the things she thought Adam should take to Sam's intended new son. Adam tried to tell her that Millie and the boy didn't need all this stuff, but he wouldn't be surprised if Mrs. Reagan wasn't walking behind him with her six boys carrying more things to his house. He was the grand marshal of a potty parade, not the respected marshal of Clear Creek.

Finally reaching his front porch, Adam stomped up the porch steps and set the high chair down so he could open the door. He turned the door knob, flung the door open—and jumped a foot off the porch floor when the toddler streaked past him, screaming at the top of his lungs—and buck naked. Good golly, now what will the townspeople think of their marshal?

Adam stepped back, expecting Millie to run past him next to sprint after the kid. After a few seconds he looked inside his house and saw no one, but he could hear female voices in the backyard.

He looked back to follow the path of the boy and realized he wasn't in sight. Adam bolted off the porch not bothering to use the steps, frantically searching for the kid as he jogged down the street. He hated to have people hear him calling for the kid—if Adam could remember his name—but he didn't think the kid would answer anyway. The boy seemed almost scared of him, but then Adam was a stranger.

Adam closed his eyes, with relief, and embarrassment. The boy was standing in front of the mercantile, petting—no, more like slapping—Henry Barclay's old dog, who always laid at his master's feet while Henry and his old friend Homer Johnston sat on the bench outside the store. And of course there were another five people standing around laughing at the child's antics because it was a busy Saturday morning, as people were coming into town to do their weekly shopping.

"Okay, fun's over everyone. I think this runaway citizen needs to be rounded up and carted off." Adam tried to be official about it, but that was hard to do when the kid shrieked at the top of his lungs and dodged out of Adam's path again.

He scooped the child up on a run and kept jogging back to his house, trying to get out of sight of everyone on Main Street. Adam slowed to a walk when he reached his porch. Just as he reached for the door handle, he felt a warm liquid running down the side of his body. He jerked the toddler back to see a little stream coming from the boy's front.

Oh great, I've just been peed on...

***

"Tate? Tate?" Millie called to the boy, realizing he wasn't in the bedroom sleeping when she went to check on him. She and Sarah had set up the wash tub in the backyard to wash clothes while Cate took her grocery list to the store. Now they were bringing in wood for the cold stove in the kitchen to fire it up to heat water for the washing.

"Was Tate just wearing a diaper when you laid him down for a nap?" Sarah asked as she pointed through the kitchen door to where a soiled diaper was lying in the middle of the living room rug.

"Oh my word! The door's open! Where is he?!" Millie panicked running into the living room just as Adam stepped into the house, his mouth set hard and his eyes shooting bullets at her.

"Your *son*, was running *naked* a whole *block* from here!" Adam spoke through gritted teeth—as Tate howled and reached for Millie.

How did mothers handle one child, let alone a full house of them? Millie was just as frustrated as Adam, but she didn't have the luxury to just hand Tate over to someone else like he was doing now.

Cate came through the front door next, looking first at Millie holding Tate, and then at her glaring son—who was holding his arm away from his wet right side. "That was quite a show you and Tate put on, Adam," she said as the corners of her mouth turned up.

"He should not be out running around, *naked*, Ma!" Adam glared as he pointed at Tate with his left hand, since his right was still holding out straight from his side.

“Oh, lighten up Adam. I can’t remember the number of times you three boys ran around *naked* outside when you were little.”

“But we lived out in the country, not the middle of town! He could have been run over by a wagon…or….”

“You could have been embarrassed running after him?”

“And he peed on me!” Adam blurted out, his face so red Millie thought he’d explode.

Cate and Sarah were laughing so hard their eyes were tearing up. “I…I remember the first time you squirted your father, Adam,” Cate tried to talk between bursts of giggles. “He was leaning over your little body with his mouth open saying ‘ah’ and you…” Cate laughed so hard tears run down her face.

“Ma…” Adam closed his eyes and hung his head, embarrassed, thinking of himself doing that.

Cate walked over and hugged her son around his waist, not worried at all about his wet shirt. “It’s just one of the joys of raising children, Adam. It’s a big responsibility, but a parent has to relish the good as well as take care of the bad…and the wet and the smelly. Yes, Tate could have been hurt, but he wasn’t and you and Millie will know now to always keep the front door locked.”

“It was shut. I just opened the door to walk in and he streaked past me.”

“And so you also learned today that toddlers move really fast.” Cate patted the front of his shirt. “How about you change your shirt so Millie can wash it with her boy’s things?”

Adam turned on his boot heel and stomped up the stairs to his room like a mad teenager.

"See what you have to look forward to as Tate grows, Millie? All stages of stubborn." Cate smiled as she saw her adult son go up the stairs. "Now while your boy is *naked*, as Adam kept saying, let's get him in the wash basin to clean him up and into a fresh diaper. The groceries will be delivered after lunch.

Thanks be again to Saint Catherine, or simply Cate. How was Millie so lucky to cross paths with her and her family?

***

This time Adam tiptoed down the stairs and eased out the front door and porch steps, trying to get away from the house before his mother found more things for him to do for his two unwanted houseguests. He had a job to do, and he tried to walk with authority down Main Street, past the people still standing and talking on the boardwalk.

Where was law and *un-order* when he needed it? Apparently not in Clear Creek at the moment. The drunks were home sleeping off last night's liquor, and there were no runaway horses and wagons to chase.

Adam let himself in the jailhouse and sank into his desk chair. Then he strummed his fingers on the desk wondering what to do. Lunch was still an hour away, and he was going to eat in the café, not go back home to see what mess might ascend on him as he opened his door next time.

With a little hesitation, Adam opened the desk drawer where he had stashed Millie's letters along with the four photographs. He pulled out the string-wrapped bundle and carefully laid them on his desk. Now that he thought about it, Millie talked like she wrote, with her Irish accent and word use. He studied each portrait, looking for any resemblance to Millie in them. The fourth one looked like her now that he looked closer, and the photo had the name of a Chicago photography studio stamped on the lower right end of the cardboard. But the woman in his house looked much thinner in the face and more solemn than the photo. There was no date on the back, so he didn't know how old it was. With the fire two years ago Adam doubted her family escaped with more than the clothing on their backs. He guessed she had a portrait taken when she started looking to become a mail-order bride.

The door opened and his brother Jacob walked in and plopped down in the chair in front of the desk. *Dang it.* He got caught looking at Millie's things again.

"Don't need to pine for the woman anymore, Adam. I hear she's living with you now," Jacob teased.

"What are you doing in town?" Adam asked, ignoring Jacob's remark. "Ma and Sarah have already badgered me today and it's not even noon yet."

"Well, in all this week's commotion, I forgot to buy Rania's wedding ring," Jacob sheepishly confessed.

"Glad to hear I'm not the only Wilerson who's having problems today," Jacob uttered as he shuffled through the envelopes on his desk. "Here's a ring for ya," he said as he tossed an envelope towards Jacob.

Jacob took the envelope and shook out the ring that was inside it. Sam had already bought Millie's ring and it was found with the letters in Sam's house. Jacob palmed the ring and looked at Adam. "It's too small. Rania tried it on when we found the letters."

The door opened again and Adam cringed when his mother walked in.

"Perfect," She said while holding out her palm to Jacob, "that's what I stopped in for." After Jacob dropped the ring in her hand, she opened up her reticule and slipped the ring inside, causing Adam to panic because…he confessed he had claimed all of Millie's things for himself as he was waiting for her to come to town.

"Why do you need the ring, Ma?" Adam asked with suspicion.

Cate sighed, but answered him willingly. "Millie has not said yet whether she should be called Miss or Mrs. I think it would be best for her reputation, since she's living with you as your housekeeper," she paused and waited for Adam's cringe to pass, "if she wears this ring and we introduce her around town as Mrs. Donovan."

His sister moved in the doorway with the little boy in her arms. It might just be his imagination, but his sister seemed more confident at carrying the kid around on her hip than Millie did.

"Where's Mille?" Adam asked his sister.

"She was exhausted, so we thought we'd take wide-awake Tate out so Millie could take a nap." *Oh yes, Tate. I have to remember the kid has a name since he's now living with me.* Sarah tickled Tate's chin and he gleefully babbled something to her. Sarah was a natural with children and Adam hoped she would have a house full—or would it be a hotel full?—of children to love and tend. That caused Adam to worry for his sister. Ethan had said more than once he wanted one son to carry on the family name, but never mentioned wanting more than one child. Ethan was the only son of his parents, and Ethan assumed that's the way it would be for him and Sarah once they were married, too.

"Adam, did you hear what I said?" His mother pulled him from his thoughts.

"Sorry Ma, what did you say?"

"Let's go, I want to eat an early lunch at the café then get back to your house to put away the groceries when they are delivered…unless you want to do that yourself." Adam looked up to see Jacob wearing his hat and standing to go.

"Come on, you just as well eat with us all while we're in town," Jacob interjected.

Adam's eyes zeroed in on the little boy in his sister's arms. How will the kid act and what will people think when seeing the child eating with Adam's family? Then he looked up at his mother, and stood, reaching for his hat. No use to balk when his mother's right eyebrow shot up.

CHAPTER 5

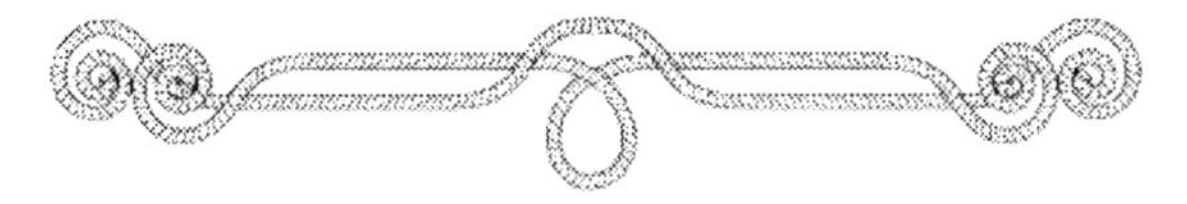

Sleep, a bath, clean clothes and attention did wonders for Tate, Adam thought. Tate smiled at his mother and his sister, at the waitress, and at every woman who stopped at their table to look the child over and gather some gossip. His shiny bright hair curled on top of his head and every woman had to stroke those locks of orange.

His mother kept offering spoonful's of mashed potatoes and gravy to the kid and he just kept eating. Adam couldn't figure out how the boy was so thin when he ate like there was no tomorrow.

At least the conversation had turned away from Tate and Millie to Jacob's wedding. Jacob was moving into the Hamner house with Rania after their ceremony tomorrow which was being held after church. Because the two houses were within a mile of each other, Jacob could take care of chores at both the Wilerson and Hamner ranches. And the newlyweds would have some privacy before Rania's parents returned from Texas. Then Jacob and Rania would move into the Wilerson house.

"We will introduce Millie and Tate to the townspeople at church tomorrow," his mother declared while holding another spoon of potatoes in front of Tate.

"Do you think Tate can sit through the service and the wedding right after that?" Sarah asked, as she gazed admiringly at the child in question.

"Hmm, I don't know if Millie attended church in Chicago and if the child was used to sitting still. Maybe we should stop back by the mercantile and see if they have a cloth book we could buy for him to look at during the service."

Adam cringed at the word "buy" because he hated to see what his account total was going to be this month. He'd have to eat at home, but then he guessed that was his mother's intention.

"Think Millie will be ready to meet everyone tomorrow? She's been through so much loss this past week. Maybe we should ask before planning her day?" Jacob asked. Adam thanked upward for another male's opinion at their table. His mother sure wasn't taking his suggestions.

"You're right, Jacob. Adam can ask Millie this evening when he comes home for supper," and his mother turned her brilliant smile on him next.

"Do you think Miss Elison will come to church with Dagmar?" Sarah leaned forward and asked. Adam thought Sarah was a bit in awe of the fancy woman who arrived from Boston last week. The woman seemed nice enough when they met last night, but Adam didn't stay long enough to really talk to her and gain an opinion.

"Who knows," Jacob said, concentrating on his chicken dinner.

"I'd hope so. She didn't say how long she was planning to visit, but you'd think she'd want to get off the ranch to visit with people. Dagmar and the ranch hands aren't the most social group to spend time with." Apparently Sarah was hoping to spend some time with this new woman in the area.

"Shall we drive by the Bar E on our way home to give her a personal invitation, Sarah?" Adam recognized his mother wanting to do something for both her daughter and the new woman. Although he internally griped about what his mother was doing for Millie and the little boy sitting on her lap, she was the best woman in the world. If Adam ever decided to marry, his bride would have to measure up to her.

"Who saved room for dessert? It's apple pie today," the waitress declared as she cleared dishes off their table.

"Both men said, "Me" at the same time before Cate and Sarah nodded yes.

"Well, Adam, Millie said she's good at making pies so you'll have to compare hers to what you're getting now," Sarah teased her brother.

"Millie will have to clean the dust off the range and the cobwebs out of the oven first. When did you last use the stove, Adam?"

"I quit carrying in wood and lighting the fire when the house was warm enough to go without heat. I get my coffee at the café in the morning so I don't bother to carry in wood and heat water."

"What about hot water for your bath? You do bathe occasionally don't you?" Sarah was on a roll now.

"Oh, I get a real good bath over at the…"

"Never mind," his mother interrupted him. "You'll start carrying wood now because Millie needs it."

If only he could eat his pie in peace...

***

Millie slowly awoke to noises coming from the kitchen through the closed bedroom door. It was the chatter of women plus a little one, all normal conversation along with the sound of water being poured into a tin tub.

When was the last time she had a chance to catch a nap? It dawned on Millie where she was, and that it was Tate making the noises in the next room.

A soft knock on the door opened Millie's eyes into the afternoon light that cast a shadow into the room. "Yes?"

"Millie, I thought you'd like a bath before we leave and Adam comes home. The tub is ready for you. We'll be in the parlor with Tate to give you some privacy."

"Thank you," Millie answered back, already feeling better than she had for days. She opened the door to find the tub full of steaming water by the stove, and towels and soap on a chair beside it. She couldn't take off her wrapper and underthings fast enough to sink into the fragrant water. Millie could tell one of the women had added a splash of Lavender Water to the tub. And it was a long enough tub to stretch her legs out in front of her instead of sitting with her knees up to her chest.

She eased into the water an inch at a time to savor the feel of heat against her skin, and so she didn't splash any water out onto the floor. It was heavenly! Millie smelled the bar of soap before rubbing it on the wash cloth she had dipped in the water. Lavender again, just what she needed to wash the smell of travel, the chicken house and the jail cot off her skin, and out of her nose.

Millie pulled up her knees and scooted down so she could dip her head under the water. Her waist-length copper-red hair floated above her in a mass of color until she pushed up her chest to surface. It had been ages since she gave her scalp and hair a good scrubbing and it felt so good.

The water had cooled before Millie rose out of the water and reached for the towel. Who knew when she'd have the luxury of a long soak again with Tate to take care of and Adam in the house at night? She knew Cate meant for her to enjoy it, so she didn't feel guilty.

How was she going to return the favor?

***

"Oh, you look like you feel so much better," Cate beamed when Millie walked into the parlor later.

"Thank you so much for heating the bath water and giving me time to enjoy it," Millie smiled back. "But I've taken so much of your time today, and you have the wedding tomorrow…"

"We had fun doing it, and having time to get to know Tate," Sarah said hugging the little boy on her lap. "But we probably should be heading on to the Bar E, don't you think, Mother?"

Cate opened up the watch pinned on her shirtwaist and agreed. "Yes, but first I have something for you, Millie, before we leave and you're on your own."

Millie swallowed hard when Cate pulled a gold band out of her reticule and handed it to her. She couldn't help when tears started forming, and tried to sniff to keep them from running down her cheeks.

"This ring was in an envelope with the letters you wrote to Sam. I assume he meant to give it to you in person…on your wedding day."

All Millie could do was nod. Sam had asked her ring size so he'd be ready for the ceremony.

Cate took the band from Millie's fingers with her left hand, and took Millie's left hand with her right. Cate looked Millie in the eyes and said, "Sam would have wanted you to have this ring—and wear it—as a symbol of his love, and as your protection until you marry again." She slid the perfect-size ring on Millie's ring finger and closed both hands around Millie's.

Millie squeezed her eyes shut, wishing Sam had been the one to put the ring on her finger instead of his neighbor. She really did enjoy his letters and was looking forward to a life with him. This symbol of his love for her hit deep in her chest, making her realize her dream of a home with Sam was shattered now.

"I'm sorry, Millie, but I knew you needed that one gift from Sam, and you also needed closure."

Millie couldn't help it when tears started running down her cheeks. After all she had gone through to get to Kansas; she still didn't have a husband or a home.

Millie was grateful when Cate gently pulled Millie into her own chest to give comfort. Why did she have to lose her husband before getting to know him, and losing the security it meant for her future too?

When she finally got control of her tears, Cate eased Millie away from her chest to look at her. "I also think you should wear the ring now and we'll introduce you as Mrs. Donovan to the townspeople. You've never said if you were married before," and Cate stopped to look at Tate, "but I think it would be best for your reputation if you say you are a widow, especially with you living in Adam's house as his housekeeper now."

Millie wiped her eyes and blew her nose on the handkerchief that Sarah handed her, and nodded in agreement. "Yes, that would be best." Millie took a deep breath to compose herself. "My husband's name was...James."

"How long were you married?" Cate asked.

"Two years, and he's been gone almost one."

"How old are you."

"I'm twenty-two." Millie caught on that Cate was helping her fabricate a story to tell people. Did Cate think she was an unwed mother?

"When is Tate's birthday?"

Millie tried to think quickly because this was the most crucial question of all. She pasted a watery smile on her face and answered, "He'll be two on June 30th."

Cate clasped her hands and smiled. "Adam will be twenty-seven on the same day! We can have a supper party for both of them at the same time."

"Mother..."

"Yes Sarah, we really do need to go. Will you be all right now, Millie?"

Millie gave Cate, and then Sarah a hug when Sarah rose off the sofa. "I can't thank you enough for all your help and support today. From the chance for some sleep, the bath, the food…"

"Well you didn't have the greeting you were expecting yesterday with Sam, so we wanted to be here for both of you." Millie had lifted Tate to her hip, and both she and Cate saw how lovingly Sarah caressed Tate's check before turning to leave.

"Oh and if Adam forgets to mention it to you, we'd love for you to join us in church tomorrow for the Sunday service and the wedding ceremony afterwards. And there will be a combination reception and church pot luck following that."

"I'd love to go to church. Is it Catholic by chance?"

"Clear Creek is so small we're lucky to have a church at all. Everyone in the area goes to it, no matter their faith before they moved west."

"Pastor Reagan's wife, Kaitlyn, emigrated from Dublin about five years ago. I'm sure she'd love to talk with you. We can hardly understand her Irish brogue when she gets excited."

That there was an Irish woman in town made Millie both happy and homesick. She'd try her best to make a home here—while she stayed.

CHAPTER 6

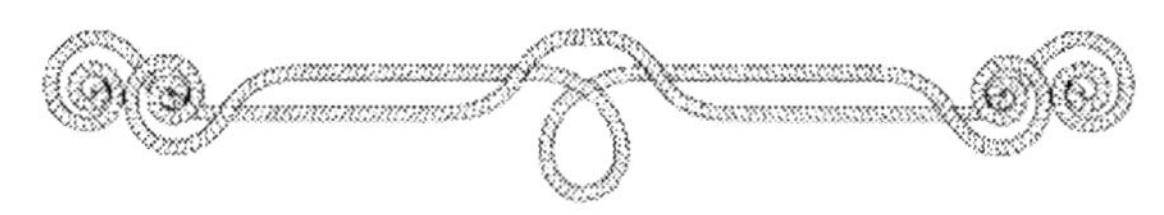

There was just polite conversation at breakfast this morning. Tate sat in his borrowed high chair, babbling and playing with the small pieces of toast and jelly that was on the high chair's tray.

The fluffy scrambled eggs, crisp bacon and light pancakes Millie made for breakfast was fit for a king, let alone a marshal. And how could she make coffee taste so good?

Last night Adam had skipped coming home for supper. Instead, he ate at the café and spent the evening making the rounds about town—several times. When he came home to a quiet, dark house, the smell of baked pies almost made him light a lamp and find a fork. But he didn't want Millie to know he was in the kitchen, so he quietly went upstairs.

He couldn't sit across the table from her last night after almost walking in on her bath yesterday afternoon. His cheeks still reddened at the thought. Luckily she had just closed her eyes to dunk her hair in the tub so she didn't know he was staring at her fine body through the door's window. Oh gosh, that swirl of wavy, red hair on her head…Adam felt like he needed to take off his hat and fan his face—but he couldn't—because he was carrying a cloth-covered pie tin in each hand for the meal after the wedding ceremony. He had to get that picture out of his head because he couldn't sleep last night, and she was living in his home, even though it was in the downstairs bedroom.

They were walking the three blocks to church now and he glanced sideways as Millie took another deep breath. Adam didn't blame the woman for being nervous. He'd had time to think about her situation and realize how overwhelming the loss of Sam and his home must be for Millie. And to have lost a sister the week before? Adam squeezed his eyes shut thinking what if his sister Sarah had died a few days ago. He really was sorry for their first meeting and how he reacted. Probably why he let his mother move her and the kid into his house.

Adam hadn't picked up the boy since their "naked dash home" as his sister called it, but Tate was always watching, almost judging Adam for his actions. At least the boy wasn't screaming his head off anymore. Not a peep out of him overnight until breakfast, and now his mouth was sucking his thumb like he hadn't eaten anything yet today.

"Clear Creek's citizens are the good decent sort, and you'll do fine meeting them," Adam announced, trying to calm Millie's nerves.

"I'm sure they are. It's just that…everything is different here compared to Chicago. The town is out in the open and without a tree in sight to hide behind—or get any shade," she added quickly. "You can easily see the end of Clear Creek from any street, and then it's nothing…"

"Nothing but beautiful, open grass and blue sky to me. I like the vast openness, nothing to capture me and hold me down."

Millie kept strolling, looking down the street to the open prairie beyond. "I must confess I've never been outside the city limits of Chicago until this trip. The train ride across the open sections of the country was intimidating to me, save for the fact that I was enclosed in the safety of the train car."

Adam turned to Millie and almost stopped with a thought. "But you were going to live out in the country with Sam. You think being in a town looking out is different…" He was going to say intimidating because that's what Adam was afraid the open countryside was to Millie.

"I know," Millie said looking down at the dirt street. "I just…I just was intent on escaping the poverty, looking for a family to love, not thinking of the different type of land or house I'd be living in," she ended softly.

"Would you like to see Sam's house, or would it be too painful? I ask that because the question is going to come up with the Hamners owning in now."

Adam could see Millie rubbing her thumb on the wedding band now circling her ring finger as she thought about his question. "Yes, I think I need to see it, because of all the 'what ifs' that continue to run through my head. Do you think they'll mind?"

"Give the newlyweds a few days to settle in, and then I'm sure Rania would love to have you visit." Adam wanted to give Millie's shoulders a hug for reassurance, and he couldn't help thinking about the creamy shoulders he saw during her bath. Jeepers, he had to clean out his mind. Good thing they were going to church.

Millie stopped and stared. "Is there a woman, and a bunch of boys running toward us?"

"Oh, brace yourself. Mrs. Reagan just heard you're Irish."

***

Millie took a deep breath, then another before taking the first step down the church aisle. Kaitlyn Reagan's joyful excitement of meeting her and Tate caused them to be late arriving to church. The preacher's wife just smiled at her husband's look of "I'm waiting for you to start the service" as she herded her family into the front left pew in front of the simple pulpit.

Adam pointed to his family sitting on the right side of the aisle, also in the front pew. There were two seats left on the center end—for them, she guessed. Millie didn't know if the Wilersons always sat in the front of the church, or they were doing so this morning because of today's wedding.

It was a simple wooden rectangle church, unpainted, with plain windows instead of stained-glass. So different from the stone cathedral in Chicago where she used to worship. Millie hurried down the aisle, shifting Tate to her left hip so she could grab the pew back. She curtsied before entering the pew, and then made the sign of the cross on her chest when seated.

When Millie opened her eyes, she was taken aback by the look of confusion in Adam's face as he slowly eased into the pew beside her. Oh gracious, she wasn't in a Catholic church, but automatically did the ritual she'd done since a child. From now on she would have to do the act in her mind only instead of physically.

She could feel the whole congregation's eyes on her back as she settled Tate in her lap. Cate sat on her right and patted Millie's arm in reassurance so Millie tried to calm her red face and concentrate on the pastor beginning the service.

"I want to welcome everyone to our service. Are there any guests today?"

Millie's eyes widened when she realized Pastor Reagan was looking directly at her. Cate stood, and touched Millie's elbow, signaling for her to stand up, too.

"I'd like you to welcome our new town residents, Mrs. James Donovan and her son, Tate. They are from Chicago and friends of the Wilerson family. Mrs. Donovan is Marshal Wilerson's new housekeeper."

Millie sat down quickly while soft murmurs from the congregation drifted to her ears. Adam felt stiff beside her, staring ahead, not acknowledging his "new housekeeper".

Well, like it or not, Cate handled the introduction for her. Now it was up to herself to blend in to the new community. Millie concentrated on the pastor's voice because she needed his words to calm her mind *and* her soul.

***

Adam rose next to her when the pastor asked for the wedding party to come forward. Solemnly he straightened his back, walked a few steps to the front and stood next to Jacob as his brother's witness. Rania's sister Hilda moved excitedly in place beside the bride, and then everyone listened to the simple wedding ceremony as Jacob and Rania exchanged vows.

Rania looked calm and utterly beautiful listening to the words of the ceremony. She was as tall as Jacob and looked straight into the adoring eyes of her groom. The sun shone through the simple church glass windows, looking as though the heavens were blessing their union.

"I, Jacob take you Rania to be my wife, to have and to hold from this day forward, for better or for worse, for richer, for poorer, in sickness and in health, to love and to cherish; from this day forward until death do us part."

Millie choked, realizing it could have been, no it *should have been* Sam telling her those words today. Tears silently moved down her cheeks as Millie thought of her loss. She felt Cate lift squirming Tate out of her tight hold just as he was about to protest her squeezing him. Cate calmly put a finger across her closed lips, and then did it to Tate's to indicate he should be quiet. Then Cate pulled a soft cloth book out from under her skirt and handed it to Tate. Millie felt even worse that she hadn't brought anything along to keep Tate quiet, but thankful that Cate had filled in again for her own lack of maternal instincts.

Through her tears, Millie watched Adam sharply turn his head when Tate talked, but his eyes softened when seeing her tear-stained face. Maybe Adam had some compassion for her situation after all.

CHAPTER 7

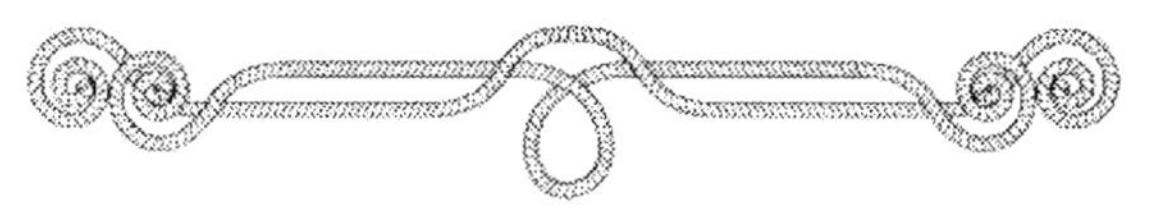

"Sarah, those were both great pies." Adam actually wiped his finger across the plate to get the very last bit of apple filling. He sucked it off his finger, and then wiped his mustache with his cloth napkin. "I don't know which one was better, the apple or the rhubarb. I had to have a piece of both."

"I didn't make them, Adam."

"Really? Well they sure weren't Mrs. Clancy's pies. I avoided them when I saw hers being unwrapped. I'll eat them in their café, but I know there are bakers in this congregation who are better than her by far."

Adam looked across the picnic table, first at his sister and then Hilda as they giggled at his remark. "What?" Then he looked to Millie on the end of the table. She was blushing, but had a funny grin on her face.

Oh no. Were these the pies I carried from my own kitchen?

"You know," Ethan put his elbows in the table and leaned forward to look at Millie, "we haven't found a baker yet for the new restaurant we'll have in the hotel. These were excellent pies and I'd like to taste some of your rolls and cakes next. I bet they would be wonderful too. Would you be interested in applying for the job, Millie?"

"Oh, that's a good idea, Ethan!" Sarah said beaming at Tate—instead of Ethan—while feeding another spoonful of apple filling into Tate's upturned mouth. Sarah held Tate throughout the entire dinner, much to Ethan's chagrin.

"I'd love to…but what would I do with Tate?" Millie quickly asked as an afterthought.

"True. He can't come to work with you," Ethan admitted, crossing his arms.

"Why not?" Sarah challenged him.

"A child in the kitchen would distract the workers, and he'd be in danger of hurting himself on the stove or utensils."

"It's no different than a mother cooking at home," Sarah shot back.

Adam watched this volleying of words back and forth with interest. Sarah had never challenged Ethan before, but she did now while hugging Tate. Maybe thinking of children would make Sarah cancel her engagement to Ethan, which would please Adam—and the rest of his family.

"The hotel's opening is still a month away, so how about if first, Millie bakes items you and your parents had planned for the restaurant's menu? She can make them at Adam's and you can pay for them as the customer would in your restaurant. You can work out Tate's care after you try her baked goods." Cate hadn't sat at their table during the picnic, but had heard the conversation and walked over to put in her suggestion.

"Pies this good would pull customers away from Clancy's, so I'm tempted to hire someone to take the kid off your hands." Ethan winked at Millie, but it didn't give her any thrill. She was worried enough that Tate would disappear from her watch as it was.

"Don't look, but we need to 'rescue' Dagmar from Miss Elison," Hilda said in a low whisper. "Millie, you haven't met my brother yet, so how about you join me in saving his neck?"

"But I have Tate…"

"Go on," waved Sarah. "Ethan and I can watch him for you." Adam tried hard to keep from smirking at Ethan's shocked expression. He was proud of his sister finally finding her backbone. He'd love for Tate to pull one of his "almost two" tantrums to see how Ethan would react.

Adam stood up, moving around the bench as he said, "I'll escort you ladies over to their table. I didn't get to visit with Miss Elison much last Friday evening, so this would be my chance now. And a chance for you two love birds to play 'family' with Tate." Adam tried to be very sincere about his kind gesture, but Sarah gave him a devilish grin and a slight nod of thanks.

Adam paused when he thought of the main reason he wanted to go along with the women. He didn't want Dagmar to get too interested in Millie. *Why am I feeling possessive of my housekeeper all of a sudden?*

***

Cora Elison was gracious and beautiful, Millie thought. Even though the petite, chestnut-haired woman wore expensive clothing, her manner was warm and friendly. Dagmar Hamner had yet to speak a word in the conversation, except to mutter a stuttering "hello" to Millie.

With ease, Cora explained how her parents bought the Bar E Ranch in Kansas to move her two brothers, Lyle and Carl, out of Boston's high roller society. They thought running a ranch would be a good experience for their sons—to give them a purpose in life.

Cora went on to say that last month her father made a surprise visit to the ranch and found the place was being used as a race track and gambling den for his sons and their friends. Mr. Elison sent the sons home and hired Dagmar to manage the ranch. The tall Swedish brother of Rania and Hilda had worked in Texas and was capable of working the Bar E cattle ranch.

The way the Wilerson family had talked, she expected Dagmar to be an easy-going, talkative man. But Millie guessed that Cora's arrival had thrown him into a tailspin.

"I was glad to see you in Clear Creek today, Cora. What do you think of the ranch and town?" Hilda asked.

Cora smiled and sighed. "I must admit I grew up in Boston's high society, but I love the open spaces of the Kansas prairie. I'd love to live here permanently."

Millie watched as Dagmar stiffened at hearing Cora's news. Thinking Chicago and Boston would be similar as established cities, she had to ask, "Why, when Boston can offer you so much more than Clear Creek can?"

For an instant Millie felt a ping of jealousy when Adam smiled at Cora. But it would make sense that Adam would be interested in Cora because she said she liked it here, when Millie had just said this morning *she* wasn't comfortable with the open prairie.

"You wouldn't think looking at my refined, regal mother that she grew up in a trading post in the Wyoming Territory." Cora smiled seeing the shocked faces of her audience. "Mother has always told me stories of her days out in the openness of the West. I've always longed to see the prairie for myself, and it became possible with the purchase of the Bar E."

"How in the world did your parents meet?" Millie asked.

"My grandparents were in Boston, and decided they wanted an adventure, so they were some of the first who traveled west on the Oregon Trail. The trip wasn't at all what my grandmother expected. She refused to go past Fort Laramie when she saw the mountain range in the distance. The trading post was their home until my grandfather died when my mother was eighteen. She and my grandmother traveled back to Boston, and my parents met and fell in love."

"But what would you do with your time living out on the range?" Millie was still stumped at the appeal of what lay beyond Clear Creek's boundaries.

Cora sighed while looking at the prairie that started just past the church built on the edge of town. "Ride, rope and enjoy the view."

"Cora, has Dagmar had you out riding the herd yet?"

Millie turned to look at Hilda when she asked that. *Wasn't that the ranch hands' job?* thought Millie?

"I'm afraid I haven't ridden yet. I don't have an English sidesaddle and will have to wait until the mercantile can order one."

Hilda stared at Cora in disbelief. "You're out in the frontier now Cora, so you need to be riding astride on a western saddle. Just look in the tack room of your barn to find several. Dagmar can match up the right saddle to the horse you want to ride."

"But I don't have the right clothing to ride astride."

Millie looked in envy at Cora's attire. Her rich-looking, maroon dress had a fitted Basque bodice that ended in a crisp flare over her hips. Besides the frilly collar and lacy cuffs, the lower back of the skirt was trimmed with deep pleats and bows. The top of her skirt featured a high bustle which was the latest feature in women's fashion.

"Not a problem," Hilda assured Cora. "You can wear one of Rania's split skirts since she won't be wearing them, or riding—if Jacob has any say about it—for the next seven or so months."

"Why won't Rania be riding?" Cora asked curiously.

Hilda hesitated a moment and looked down at her hands in her lap. "Jacob and Rania are excited about her pregnancy now, but…she was attacked on the cattle trail up here by one of our cattle drivers. The man, Sid Narker, threatened harm to her family members if she told anyone. Turns out he trailed up to Ellsworth before us…"

Cora gasped. "I saw his name on the Bar E payroll when I was going through the books!"

"Yes, Narker worked there a few weeks until your father fired him. We didn't realize that he was in the area, though, until Rania heard him speaking while she was in town one afternoon."

Millie glanced over at the happy newlyweds mingling through their guests' tables. She shuddered when she thought of what

Rania went through. *Will I be happy here, or is someone following me, too?*

"Well, what happened? You've got to tell us the rest of the story now," Cora said with wide eyes.

Hilda shut her eyes and shuddered. "A little over a week ago Narker kidnapped Rania from our family's homestead and forced her to go with him on horseback. The horses had problems when crossing the flooded river…Rania and her horse Rose, nearly died, but Jacob saved them." She sighed in relief.

"What happened to Narker?"

"His horse drowned, and it was assumed Narker did too, although his body was never found. That's not unusual when things get trapped in the debris that gets jammed up in a flood," Hilda said matter-of-factly.

Millie glanced at Rania again. She thought Chicago could be dangerous, but there could be problems in this desolate place, too, apparently. Was this just the way things were out here?

"Since you're from a big city, too, do you ride, Millie?" Hilda asked. Millie shot a nervous look at everyone around the table, hating to confess, when riding a horse was the main transportation in the West.

"I'm afraid I've never sat on a horse, or driven a wagon. I've always walked or ridden in a carriage when in Chicago. My trip here was the first time I had been on a train, too."

Hilda got a gleam in her eye. "Do you either of you ladies know how to shoot a gun to defend yourself?"

Cora looked at Millie but answered for herself. "I've shot a small derringer, but nothing like the revolvers or rifles I've seen around here." Millie was familiar with her father's pistol, but had never shot a rifle so she shook her head no. *Maybe this is something I should know.*

Millie was taken aback when Hilda clapped her hands. "Wonderful! I can teach you both how to ride and shoot! It will be so fun!"

Adam said, "I'll teach Millie how to shoot…" at the exact same time as Dagmar said, "I'll teach Cora how to shoot…"

Hilda beamed with satisfaction as if she had planned that. "Fine. You men teach *your ladies* the proper way to care and shoot firearms, but I'm definitely the best woman to show them how to ride."

Adam pointed a finger at Hilda, "You are *not* going to put Millie on Nutcracker. She has a son to take care of, and Tate doesn't need to be motherless."

Millie's eyes widened with alarm, thinking about getting on any horse, let alone a dangerous one.

"My gelding is a perfect gentleman with women. It's men he hates with a passion."

"I suppose that's true, Hilda, but you have some good mares at your place or your parents', that Millie and Cora could ride instead of that nutty horse," said Adam.

Dagmar had been quiet for most of this conversation but now he spoke up, after glancing at Cora. "I think the ladies should go to Hilda's homestead, don't you Adam? It will give them a real taste of frontier living." Millie wondered why both men broke out in such large smiles.

CHAPTER 8

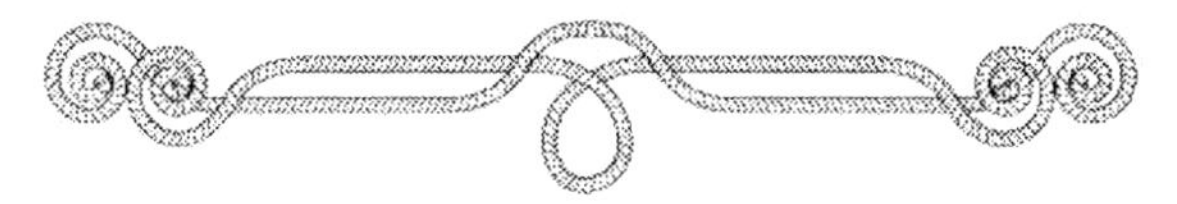

All in all, things settled down to a routine in his house. Both Millie and Tate were much more agreeable and settled after a week of decent sleep and food. Adam showed up for meals—because Millie's cooking was always mouth-watering and fabulous—and then he disappeared to the jailhouse or walked around town, occasionally riding out for business or to see his family. He tiptoed into the house late at night, after his final rounds, and up to his bedroom so he wouldn't disturb—or see—them.

Millie was getting used to small town life. Now, driving Tate and her out to Hilda's homestead, Adam couldn't wait for Hilda's sod house to come into view. He would bet Dagmar was relishing Cora's first gasp at the crude house too, as he was driving her out at the same time. Sarah had volunteered to come over to take care of Tate while the women had their first riding and shooting lessons. Adam chuckled to himself, betting his mother wouldn't miss the "show" either.

Both his passengers stared, wide-eyed and quiet, at the open scenery. Adam couldn't figure out why it seemed to bother Millie, but it did. Heck, this way it was hard for anyone to sneak up on you, but she got that "frightened deer" look in her eyes after he mentioned that fact.

"Here we are, Hilda's home sweet home," Adam announced as he pulled the horse's reins and then set the brake on the buggy.

"Dirty house," Tate exclaimed, pointing at the soddie.

"Yes, Hilda lives in a sod house made of grass and soil layers. There are no trees on the prairie for wood, so you have to make your dwelling out of what is available." Adam jumped from the buggy and walked around to help the others down. He swung Tate down to the ground and watched as he toddled toward Hilda, who stood outside her home holding a tiny, yapping dog. Hilda's dog should keep Tate busy and vice versa. That mutt was never quiet.

Adam automatically turned, ready to help Millie down, but she stayed seated, looking around the place instead of at his waiting hands. "Come on, it'll be all right. You really do need to learn how to ride and shoot if you stay in Kansas."

"Did Hilda dig...or build this house by herself?" Millie asked as she finally rose.

"No, although I'm sure she'd be up to the task. My other brother, Noah, claimed this acreage and built the house and buildings before he went back East to get his bride."

"What happened—since he isn't here, and Hilda owns the place instead?"

Adam's hands tingled in delight at having them around Millie's slim waist and he hesitated to let go of her after he got Millie down to the ground. "Huh? Oh, Noah's intended had already married someone else before he got there, and he's been roaming the West since then. Hilda bought the place since Noah hadn't proved up the claim yet."

Dagmar and Cora pulled up in the ranch buggy, and Cora jumped out and ran towards the house before Dagmar got the startled horse under control. Adam watched Dagmar shake his head and probably say "Dang". Cora chatted excitedly to Hilda while she patted the sod bricks that made up the house.

"Looks like Cora's settling into the *Wild West*?" Adam asked Dagmar as they walked their horses toward the barn to unhitch the buggies.

"She has taken to the ranch better than a baby duck to water. First she spent hours roping a fence post. Then she moved on to roping the poor ranch dogs. She caught a running horse yesterday, and about got drug off her own mount until she finally let go of the rope.

"Cora begged a pair of trousers from a smitten ranch hand and has been riding a different horse each day, going all over the ranch with anybody who is going anywhere. She even spent yesterday afternoon out riding the herd. Riding astride in a western saddle has not been a problem for her. Actually, she's quite a horsewoman, but don't you dare repeat that, Adam Wilerson."

Adam couldn't help but tease, "So how's living together going?"

"She hadn't unpacked the first of *five trunks* that the hands lugged upstairs by the time I moved out of the big house and was settled in to the bunk house. Why would you need so much stuff and outfits for just a visit? Can you imagine what she would have brought along if she was actually moving here?" Dagmar's voice rose with each sentence.

"At least you don't have to worry anymore about all that fancy crystal in the house that you patrolled watch over every night," Adam couldn't resist kidding the tall Swede as Dagmar took a playful swing at him.

"So you been eating her cooking?"

"Nope. Been eating with the ranch hands, as has Cora. I must say she's made herself right at home. Not an uppity bone in her body. Reuben Shepard, our 'chief cook and bottle washer' has even warmed up to her."

"She trying to take over the ranch management since her father owns it?"

Dagmar twitched his mouth back and forth before answering. "You know I was worried about that, but so far all she's done is look through the account ledgers and just politely ask questions. She still hasn't said a word about her family or why she's out here by herself.

"At least you don't look scared to death of her anymore," Adam said, and Dagmar hung his head and blushed.

"Yea, I'm finally feeling more at ease around her. Cora's okay for a rich, city girl."

"Glad to hear you're getting along. How about we set up a shooting range west of the barn after we take care of the horses? Between ours and Hilda's variety of guns, the ladies can get the feel of several different types of weapons."

***

Millie's hands shook and her breath quickened as she walked out of the dirt house and over to where the rest of the people stood by the corral. She had gone inside Hilda's one-room house to change into Rania's split skirt. Even though the dirt floor, dirt walls, and the ceiling, made with limbs and dirt, was made out of….dirt…it still looked and smelled cleaner than most buildings and streets in the part of Chicago where she had lived. Everything was such a contrast from her past life.

I can do this. I have to do this. Millie told herself as she took deep breaths and willed her feet to walk over to the waiting horse that looked curiously her way. Millie hoped it wasn't the famed Nutcracker that everyone had talked about earlier.

Hilda handed Millie a slice of apple when she got close to her new friends.

"Millie, hold your palm out flat and steady and let Louise eat this apple slice. Her funny nose hairs will tickle your palm, but she won't bite you…if you keep your hand flat."

Millie couldn't keep her hand from shaking until Adam took her by the elbow and steadied her in front him at the horse's head. "It's okay, Millie. Hilda trains her animals to be calm and gentle. There's no reason to be scared of this little mare."

"But she's taller than me and could stomp on my foot," Millie barely whispered. She couldn't help leaning back on Adam to soak in his support and the strength of his warm chest.

Cora was already sitting comfortably on a brown and white blotchy looking horse that she thought Hilda had called a palomino paint. "Just relax Millie, and talk to her," encouraged Hilda.

Oh dear. Cora is already at ease on top of a horse, and I'm afraid to stand near one?

Millie's brain scrambled to take in what Hilda was saying. "…just put your boot in the stirrup and swing your right leg over to the other side. Adam will steady you, so don't be afraid."

She took a deep breath and did as she was told, with the help of Adam's guidance. He patted her leg and said, "Now open your eyes and keep them open." Millie realized she did have her eyes squeezed shut and opened them to stare at Adam's twinkling, hazel eyes.

Hilda had a hold on the mare's reins. "Okay, Millie. Hold on to the pommel, that's the horn-shaped piece on the front of the saddle, and I'll lead you around for a bit first so you can get your balance."

Millie couldn't help panicking, seeing how high she was off the ground, so she decided to stare ahead at the scenery instead. Adam kept his hand on her thigh to help keep her balanced, although it made Millie's nerves tingle instead. She willed her attention off the man and onto the horse because she needed to learn how to ride. Besides it being a way of life here, Millie might need to know how to ride should she ever need to escape danger.

***

Overall, Adam thought the morning's lessons of riding and shooting had gone well. Cora knew how to ride, but Millie knew how to shoot, it turned out. After Millie got comfortable with the weight and length of each weapon, she picked off the targets like a pro. When asked about her knowing how to shoot, she just answered that her father had instructed her when she was a child.

It was fun to watch Dagmar lean over, almost in half because of his height, to put his arms around petite Cora to steady the rifle for her. Hilda and Adam made eye contact and then rolled their eyes in unison, because they both knew that Cora was leading Dagmar on with her helpless act. Adam would bet a month's salary that Cora could shoot a jumping prairie dog at twenty yards away, but she seemed to miss every target on purpose so Dagmar would "help" her with the next shot.

Adam's mother had shown up with a picnic lunch that they enjoyed while sitting on blankets in the shade of the barn. And the meal was topped off with a mouth-watering slice of Millie's Sunshine Cake. The Paulson's had received the angel food cake that Millie had used eleven egg whites to make. Adam wished he could have tasted that, but he was satisfied when Millie used the egg yolks for the cake they had just eaten. He was going to get fat—and spoiled—on her delicious baked goods. Millie was going to get the hotel's baking job, if they could come up with a plan for someone to take care of Tate.

Tate was warming up to Adam, even though they didn't talk much. The star still bothered Tate for some reason. Adam figured out he could pick the boy up, if he took his badge off and stuck it in his pocket first.

The relationship between Millie and her boy seemed odd to him at times, not the usual bond he'd seen between a mother and child. Maybe that was because of their home situation before coming to Kansas, but neither talked about Tate's father, and supposedly Millie's husband.

Twice this week Adam found Tate visiting with Henry and Homer in front of the mercantile. At least both times Tate was fully clothed. Luckily the old men had appointed themselves as Tate's unofficial babysitters. Tate wandered off as Millie got caught up in her baking, forgetting about him until thirty minutes later when she'd coming running down the street calling for him.

There was something else that Adam wondered about. He would ask Tate, "Where's your momma?" and the child would look around, tears forming in his baby blue eyes. When Adam asked where Millie was, Tate would point toward the house. Part of the time Tate called Millie "Illie" instead of "momma" too.

Adam, as the town marshal, had gotten a wire from St. Louis asking if a young woman named Donovan, and a red-haired boy had arrived safely in Clear Creek. It wasn't signed, which wasn't unusual to save on the cost of a wire. Adam answered back right away as he was requested. Millie didn't talk about her family. Her mother and siblings had all passed, and it sounded like the father didn't have a presence in her life. Adam guessed the brother-in-law wanted to be sure Millie made it to her new home so he was the one who sent the wire.

He didn't know how single mothers like Millie made it in this world. And, he couldn't help feeling a little bit of satisfaction knowing he was helping them both out. Adam felt blessed to have a close family and a good set of neighbors.

Adam watched Tate toddle by with Hilda's little mutt yipping at his heels. Maybe he'd get Tate a pet—but definitely something quieter than Hilda's. Jacob brought in a dozen hens to Adam's chicken house the first of the week so Millie would have fresh eggs, and darned if Tate didn't capture one of the squawking chickens and carry it down to show Henry and Homer. Adam chuckled to himself, thinking of that scene he had come across.

Everyone was enjoying themselves, but it was time for Adam to return to town. And he had also learned that it was best if Tate took a nap in the early afternoon. Only a week ago he was a carefree bachelor, immersed in the protection of Clear Creek.

Why today, am I thinking about a child's nap time instead?

CHAPTER 9

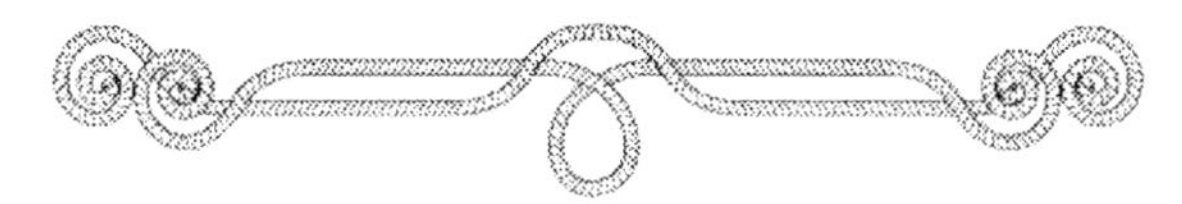

Millie, elbow deep in hot dishwater, looked out the kitchen window, watching Tate chase the kitten he and Adam had picked out yesterday from the neighbor's latest cat litter. She'd have to rescue the poor little cat soon. Even though Adam patiently showed Tate how to be careful with the "baby", it was going to need a nap, just like Tate. Adam had fenced in a section of the backyard so at least she didn't have to worry about Tate escaping now—until he was old enough to figure out how to open the gate latch.

Two weeks had done wonders for Tate's weight and acceptance of his new life. The toddler was a chubby happy boy now, enjoying the simple pleasures of life and the people who doted on him. Tate still he fussed at night, but never asked about his father.

Millie thanked her lucky stars every day. The Wilerson women and Hilda stopped to visit when they were in town, plus women from the church welcomed her, even if she was living with the marshal. Cate's announcement that she was a widow had nipped any gossip in the bud.

Millie caught herself wishing—no pretending—that Adam was her husband coming home for lunch soon instead of just the town marshal she worked for.

What would it feel like for Adam to come in the back door, hug her from behind when she stood at the sink and give her neck a kiss? Would the kiss tickle? What sweet words would he whisper in her ear?

Millie remembered her parents doing just that sort of thing when she was young. It made her feel loved and secure, and Millie wished Tate could see that kind of relationship between parents as he grew up. He needed that solid foundation to build his own future.

***

Sam had described his farm to Millie in his letters, but it was a harsh reality to finally see it in person. Jacob and Rania had invited the family to their home after church today, of course including her and Tate. Millie sensed this dinner was planned for her to finally see the place she would have called home. Adam pulled the buggy near the house, but didn't talk or get down. He sensed what an emotional moment this was for her.

This would have been my house. Millie slowly looked at the outline of the one-story home, the placement of the door and windows; wondering what it would have felt like to wash their glass, look out them to see Sam's and her children playing, watch storms roll over the prairie, see Sam walk toward the door at the end of his day.

Other than the house, there was a small barn with corrals around it and a chicken house. Millie tried to tell herself this was like visiting any homestead, until she spied the row of tiny twigs with a few leaves on each one, planted in a straight line on the north side of the house.

Sam had promised he would plant trees for Millie as soon as spring allowed. The saplings were so tiny, but he'd fulfilled his promise to her. She couldn't help it when a whimper escaped her choked-up throat. This was supposed to be *her* home, *her* new start of a happy life with a loving man and their healthy children. *Why did Sam have to die?*

She couldn't see through her tears when someone reached for Tate and took him from her lap. But she felt Adam's strong arms gently gather her into his chest, surrounding her with sympathy and concern. Oh what would she have done if the Wilersons hadn't taken her and Tate into their fold? *I would have been alone and penniless in a little Kansas town.*

She wasn't sure how long Adam held her until her weeping subsided. Millie pulled away from Adam, immediately feeling the loss of his warmth and compassion, but she had to face the rest of the tour of the place. She knew tears would fall when they arrived at her—*no, she needed to remember to think of it as the Hamner home*—so she had her handkerchief already balled up in her hand to wipe away the tears that streaked her cheeks.

"I'm going to be all right now." She looked past Adam, realizing the whole family stood quietly with compassion as she faced the final blow of Sam's death.

She had to sniff up a tear, but she turned to Rania, "Thank you for having me out here today." Millie then looked to each member of the family, "And thanks to all of you for your support. I needed to see where I would have lived, but I'm glad we waited. I've gotten to know Sam's wonderful neighbors first."

Cate signaled for her and Adam to get down from the buggy. "Let's finish the tour of the place, then you can put the past behind you. Life has other things in store for you, and I'm sure they are just as good."

Yes, Millie thought as she felt Adam's hands around her waist, something just as good might be in town, if only a certain marshal would consider marrying her.

Millie couldn't help but compare Adam's house to this house as the women walked through it together. The small rooms had a minimal amount of plain furniture, just what you'd expect from a bachelor furnishing a homestead house. Sam told her she could do whatever she wanted to make it a home once she arrived, but now she couldn't think of what she would do, *or would have done.*

Adam's house had become her home in two short weeks, and she thought of feminine touches she'd like make there in certain areas. Instead of blushing, thinking of being with Sam in his bedroom, she was thinking of Adam's room upstairs in his house. The bedroom across the hall from Adam's room would be perfect for a nursery during the night when they were upstairs, and she could use the downstairs room off the kitchen as their baby's day room.

Oh, dear. Millie was appalled that she was thinking of another man while viewing her fiancé's home. *When had she fallen in love with Adam?*

"Come see 'eep an' little horsey!" Tate yelled as he rushed in the front door, plowing into Millie's knees as she walked back into the front room of the house.

"I believe Tate's met my flock," Rania chuckled. "Shall we continue the tour to the barn next, Millie?"

Millie took in the simple shed where a few chickens scratched in the dirt around the structure. The barn was two-story, to accommodate hay storage above the lower section of stalls. She knew that much about barns after she and Tate had crawled into the hayloft of Boyer's livery barn, twice, their first night in Clear Creek.

Jacob caught Tate as he rushed toward the three animals where the men were standing. "Here Tate. Now you can ride King. Hold on to his fur, but don't kick him with your feet. You have to sit real still, okay?"

Oh, what a sight! Tate sat on the back of the largest white dog Millie had ever seen, Jacob walked beside them, ready to steady Tate when he was sure to slide off… with two sheep trailing behind the trio.

"Will show Momma!"

"Yes, you'll have to show your mother the dog and sheep when she gets here…"

Millie froze as everyone turned to stare at her. *Oh. No.* She'd been worried about Tate letting their secret slip—and she had just done it herself.

Millie watched Adam's expression change instantly from friendly to calculating and cold. It was crystal clear that the marshal did not like being deceived, especially by the woman living under his roof.

Surprisingly it was Cora who spoke up before Adam. "Tate, how about if you and I see how far King will take you into his pasture? Maybe he has a secret place he'd like to show us." Cora gave Millie a sympathetic nod and then led King away from the adults.

Tell the truth, Lassie. You know it will come out eventually. Millie pursed her lips, and sucked air into her lungs thinking of her father's words.

"I'm sorry…I let you think my sister was dead when Adam assumed it. I was trying to protect Tate."

"And Tate is…" Cate asked, but Millie guessed she had an inkling of who he was.

"My sister's son."

Millie felt Adam's eyes bore into her head, even though she didn't turn toward him. "Did Sam know you were bringing Tate with you?"

She had done nothing wrong, so she met Adam's eyes straight on. "Yes, well he would have…. Darcie asked me to take Tate with me so I wrote to Sam right away. Unfortunately, he didn't get the letter, did he?" Another thought quickly lit in her mind. "So where did the letter go if it wasn't with Sam's things?" She tried to squash the panic that threatened to grow in her chest.

"I imagine the post master sent it back to the name and address on the envelope."

"Oh no. *Oh no.* It cannot go back to Darcie's house."

"And why not?" demanded Adam.

Dots appeared in her vision as a panic attack started to develop at the thought. "Her husband always gets the mail, and he'll find out where we are."

Cate's arm across Millie's shoulders helped her regain her composure. *I have to figure this out, think this though.*

"I think it's time you tell us what's going on, Millie. Sam can't help you, but we can," Cate quietly stated as they walked back to the front porch. "Please start from the beginning."

Millie took a deep breath, looking out to Tate and Cora wandering around the pasture.

"Darcie was so happy when Curtis Robbins asked our Da, I mean our father, if he could marry her. Curtis was handsome, and Darcie assumed he was a good man, seemed to be respected by everyone." Millie paused to glance at Adam. "He…worked with my father."

"It wasn't long after they were married that Curtis became very possessive and demeaning. He was a wonderful husband when our father was around, but a different man when I was alone with them. And I feared what he was like to Darcie when I wasn't there.

"Against Darcie's protests, he decided they'd move after Tate was born. Da and I didn't know where they were for several months until Darcie's neighbor mailed a letter to me. They were in St. Louis; just far enough away we couldn't visit easily. After that, Darcie and I wrote back and forth through her neighbor."

Hilda let out an exasperated breath. "Why didn't your father go get her and Tate then?" Millie looked at Sarah and Rania, holding on to Cate's arms as they heard her story, and as usual Hilda had her fists up and ready to charge in to help.

"Da wouldn't tell me what, but Curtis had something on him or the family, something that made Da back off from getting involved in their marriage. That's when I decided to advertise as a mail-order bride out west. I'd disappear out on the frontier, and then Darcie and Tate would follow when it was safe."

"So what went wrong since Tate is with you, but not your sister?" Cate was the next person to ask a question.

"Darcie became pregnant again, and too sick to write according to the neighbor. She said to come when the baby was due so I kept working to make more money for their escape."

"So you led Sam on, planning to use his money and his home as a place for the four of you to live?" Adam ground out.

Millie met Adam's glare, getting tired of this man's accusations. "No, I did not lead him on. I would have been a loving and faithful wife to Sam. But yes, our home, *Sam's and mine,* would be a safe haven for my sister and her babies until she could get on her feet. That's what family does, right? *Wouldn't you do that for your family and vice versa?*"

CHAPTER 10

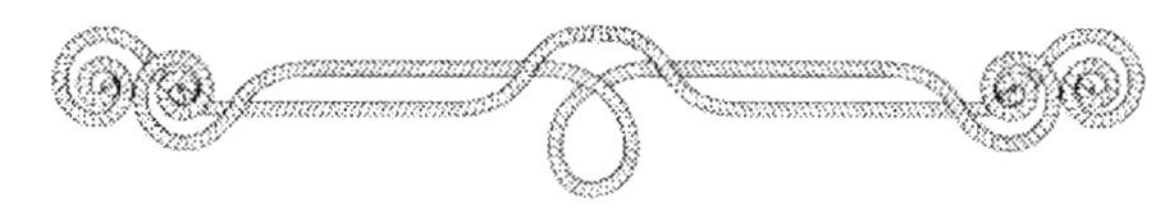

Adam lowered his glare at Millie's last question. She was right. He would help his family, and knew Millie would do the same for hers, seeing how she was covering up for her sister, pretending to be her nephew's mother while living in Clear Creek.

"I'm sorry, Millie. You're right. And Sam would have helped your family any way he could. So what happened after you got to your sister's home?"

He hated when she paused, almost at a loss for words and then she hugged herself. "I hardly recognized my sister. She was so thin, even if she was about to give birth. The left side of her face had shades of yellow shadowing it....and I'm positive her right wrist was broken it was so swollen. Tate wasn't in much better shape as you remember. Curtis ate most of his meals out, rarely bringing home decent food or giving Darcie money to go buy supplies when she felt up to it. The widow lady next door was sneaking food to them, and using her own money for Darcie's stamps for mailing the letters."

"How did Robbins act when you showed up? Or were you already gone by then?"

"He was half drunk when a friend brought him home that evening. Curtis laughed, asking what I thought of his beautiful family now. I could have beaten the man to a pulp with the fireplace poker if there would have been one in the house. The house was clear of anything Darcie could have used to defend herself against him."

"Why didn't your sister or the neighbor go to the police to report her husband?" Cate asked.

"Women and children are considered the man's property, and rarely does anyone step in to help, especially when the man in question is the law in that part of town," Millie said in disgust.

The hair on the back of Adam's neck was rising with fear. "What do you mean Millie?"

"No one is going to believe how he treats his family, because my brother-in-law is a deputy marshal in St. Louis."

Adam thought back to domestic scenes he had disrupted in Clear Creek this past year. Tomorrow he would go back and check on every woman and child in those households to be sure the fear of God and the marshal's star still protected those families from the man of the house.

"How'd you get away?"

"Darcie started going into labor, but Curtis wouldn't let her lie down in their bed, so I took her next door to the neighbor's house. After she delivered her little baby girl, Darcie begged me to take

Tate and go to Sam's as planned. The neighbor promised to move Darcie somewhere safe until Darcie is able to travel. We agreed it would be easier for me to take care of Tate instead of Darcie trying to handle both children."

"How would you know when your sister would arrive?"

"The neighbor promised to wire Sam Larson when Darcie left. And after…well finding Sam no longer here, I told the telegraph operator to look for a message to Sam—from my friend—who would tell me the date of their arrival."

Adam thought back to the telegraph he got a few days after Millie arrived. "There was a telegraph…"

"When? Is she already on her way? I didn't expect them for a month or more because of Darcie and her baby's poor conditions."

"But it just asked if you, 'Millie Donovan and a boy' had arrived, and it wasn't signed."

"It was addressed to Sam?"

"No it was addressed to the marshal of Clear Creek."

"Adam…you think this Robbins got Millie's letter back, and was confirming Millie and Tate were here with that wire?" Jacob inquired with worry. "Where did it come from?"

He rubbed the back of his neck, thinking about the wire he received and what he was afraid it meant. "The police station at St. Louis. And, I answered back that they had indeed arrived safely." The terror on Millie's face sent shivers down his spine. *What have I done? Put them in danger.*

"I'm bringing back a hungry little boy *with big ears and eyes*. Ready to eat?" Cora called out to warn the adults as Tate raced toward them.

Adam turned his attention to the laughing little boy gleefully running toward the porch. How could anyone hurt such a sweet child?

Now it all made sense. Tate was terrified of his marshal's badge because Tate's father wore one. By habit now, Adam unpinned his badge and stuck it in his vest pocket before entering the house. In the past few days Tate looked for Adam to enter the kitchen for their meals together, often playing hide and seek with him, in a two-year-old's way. Adam made funny names up just to make Tate laugh. "Sweet poo-Tater" was Tate's favorite nickname so far.

As Millie caught Tate up in her arms and hugged him tight, Adam realized why she faced all kinds of odds and sacrificed things for the child. She loved him. It didn't matter that Millie was Tate's aunt instead of his mother. She promised to take care of him, no matter what, and she was doing a fine job of it, even if the tyke ran off a few times at first.

It hit Adam hard in the chest that he loved both of them too. But he might have put them in danger by inadvertently answering a wire.

So what was he going to do about it—especially if Robbins came to town demanding his son back? Robbins had a right to take his son away from Millie, and even press charges against her.

What's right isn't always right, Adam. His father quoted that phrase over and over to Adam as he grew up, first when Adam wanted to be a soldier, then a lawman. This was surely a situation where he needed to do what was right, for a woman and child, not how the law stated. *But how am I going to legally get around that?*

"How about we eat lunch and talk again during Tate's nap?" Adam looked first at his mother, then Jacob and Dagmar. Millie had already walked by with Tate still in her arms. They had to come up with a way to protect Millie and Tate while Adam found out where and what Robbins was up to. His lawman's mind was storming up all kinds of scenarios in his head about Millie's predicament, and most of them weren't good.

***

"I wish you would have stayed out with my family, Millie."

"Absolutely not, Adam. I didn't feel safe out there. We need to be around you and a town full of people." Millie's arms were crossed in defiance and he swore there were little shots of red sparking out of her hair now and then.

"He's going to show his badge and demand Tate goes back with him."

"I don't see why. Curtis didn't want the boy in the first place, so why would he come for him now?"

Adam threw his arms in the air with his exasperation. "*Just because he can.* Mean men are that way, Millie, and I'm worried to death about both of you. I'm almost positive he'll show up when we least expect him."

"Remember I'm a cop's daughter and I do know a few things about defending myself. Your mother and sister are coming into town tomorrow and we're having a ladies meeting to let the town's women know what's going on, so they will be on alert."

"You think a bunch of ladies can take care of the law in this town? *I'm* in charge." *I thought*.

"We women can be very resourceful when prepared." Millie's chin went up a notch and another red curl sprung from her tight bun.

"So you're all going to walk around with a rolling pin, ready to swing at the man? How will the ladies know what the man looks like?"

"You have given me some thoughts I'll need to bring up at the meeting."

"Shouldn't I be involved in your meeting, so I know what the heck you have up your sleeves?"

"We decided it was best to keep you in the dark about our plan. But we'll be sure Henry and Homer know because they are the first line of defense, as the town sentries."

"Don't you mean the town's centenarians?" Adam scoffed. "Well, can I at least defend you in our home? I want you and Tate sleeping upstairs at night. He can take his naps in the downstairs room, but *I want you upstairs tonight*. No arguments."

By gosh the woman didn't have an argument back at him. Millie stared at him wide-eyed and her mouth in a perfect "O". *Oh, gosh what did I just say? Our home... I want you upstairs tonight.* Adam's face turned beet red as he spun on his boot heel and rushed out the door.

***

Millie heard Adam come in late last night, because she and Tate were in the room across the hall from his bedroom and she was wide-awake, still thinking about his statement that he wanted her "upstairs"...and how she wished she could be "upstairs" enjoying being his wife.

But then thoughts of *why* they were upstairs, because Tate was in danger, killed the mood. Now she had breakfast ready and he was stalling coming downstairs.

Millie heard Adam's boot steps come down the steps and enter the room, but didn't turn to look at him until Tate screaked in terror. She spun around then stopped, looking at Adam's bruised chin. His face had been a target for someone's fist last night.

"Tate, it's okay, Adam just has a boo-boo on his face. He doesn't even need a bandage."

"Why is he so upset?" Adam asked above the child's screams.

"Think about it, Adam..." Millie knew when Adam realized Tate had seen—and felt—bruises before.

Adam crouched down to Tate's height at the high chair. "Oh, no. I'm okay, Sweet poo-Tater, I really am. Please don't cry..."

Millie glanced at Adam, then Tate, wondering if her remedy for Tate's "boo-boos" would calm the toddler down. "Tate. Tate, don't you think Adam should have a 'Baker's Kiss' on that boo-boo?"

"Huh?" Tate stopped his crying and looked between the adults. That caused Adam to look between her and Tate in confusion as well.

"What's a Baker's Kiss, Millie?" Adam asked warily.

Millie opened the pie cupboard and took out a little tin container and a larger one from a shelf, put them on the table in front of Tate, and took off the lids.

Millie smiled at Tate and asked sweetly, "Shall I give you a Baker's Kiss first so Adam can see what they are? Where was your last boo-boo, Tate?"

Now Tate was excited, waving his left arm and pointing at it with his right hand. "Here, here!" The tot was transformed into an excited, happy child compared to the terrified boy of a minute ago.

"Okay. We take the special cookie, dip it in the special sugar, and pat the boo-boo. Then…" Millie paused to lick her tongue all over her lips, "you get the special Baker's Kiss on your boo-boo." She wet her lips again and carefully touched her puckered mouth on his skin, taking off a bit of sugar, leaving the imprint of a kiss on his arm.

Tate grinned in delight, then took the cookie from Millie's palm and stuck it in his mouth, happily chewing on the shortbread cookie.

"No wonder the kitchen smells like cookies half the time, and my socks smell like sugar if I walk in stocking feet around the kitchen. Tate's been having lots of boo-boos?" Adam quietly asked Millie.

"Oh yes, but it's become a happy game and I'm fattening him up at the same time," Millie whispered back.

"Adam's turn! Gets a kiss from Illie!"

Millie sucked in a breath to fortify her intention. There was another reason she wanted to give Adam a kiss besides to calm Tate down. She wanted to announce her feelings to Adam.

She had formed small round shortbread cookies, and pinched up a bit of dough on top before she baked them to give a little handle for her to dip into the tin of fine sugar. Millie ground sugar with a mortar and pestle to make it very fine and added a little corn starch to make the sugar stick better to the skin.

"Sit down in the chair by Tate, Adam, so he can see your kiss. What's the simple version of how you got your boo-boo, Adam?"

Millie took a cookie from the tin, dabbed it in the sugar tin, and carefully touched the bruise on Adam's chin.

"I overreacted when Ralph Peters…uh yelled at his wife, and I got a boo-boo on my chin."

"He hit you, just because of that?"

"Uh, I swung at him first without thinking and…Ida decked me."

Millie giggled and touched his chin again because the sugar fell off when Adam talked.

"Ida is twice the size of Ralph, so I'm sure she can protect herself."

"Yeah, I think of that every time I move my jaw."

"Kiss! Kiss!" Millie licked her lips as Tate started chanting. She watched Adam stare at her lips as she slowly moved towards his face. She took a breath, then gave him a long, wet, kiss right in the middle of the sugar smear.

"I think you missed the exact spot," Adam slowly smiled while looking at her sugar-covered lips."

"Oh, I know I did," Millie said as she dipped the cookie into the sugar mix and this time dabbed directly on his upturned lips. She put the cookie on the table and wrapped her arms around Adam's shoulders before lowering her lips to zero in on her target.

CHAPTER 11

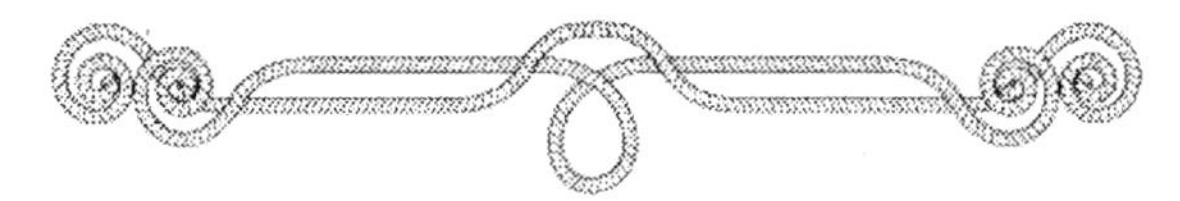

"I just Adam tried to keep his mind on the sermon, but his eyes kept glancing at Millie, thinking about all the "Baker's Kisses" they had shared in the past week, with or without the cookies, depending on whether they had a toddler's audience or not. He glanced over Millie's head to see his mother's, apparently knowing, smile. *Dang*, the preacher was probably watching him make longing glances at Millie's lips, too.

It had been a wonderful week with Mille, but an exasperating one for work. He had to keep his mind on his job and it was hard, thinking about Millie and Tate's situation. Extra cowboys in town meant extra scuffles between brands, drunks who had to sleep their stupid stupor off in the jail, and another domestic violence case when he should have arrested himself for being so brutal against the man who slapped his wife.

He also did something that he was positive would upset Millie's shooting red curls—but he did it anyway. Adam finally convinced Millie to write a letter to her father explaining the situation. The two needed to mend the rift between them, not only for their sake, but also for Darcie and her children. He said he'd deliver the letter to the post office, but instead he took it to the jailhouse, locked the door and carefully opened the letter to read what Millie had written.

He did reseal and mail the letter, after he wired Mr. Donovan in care of the Chicago Police Department. That man had a right to know what was going on with his family; and personally, Adam thought the father should be involved in protecting his daughters and grandchildren. He had to word the letter carefully, not knowing who might read it in Chicago, but he had to try contacting Millie's father.

Adam didn't worry about Clear Creek's telegrapher knowing about it, because the whole town knew Tate's story and was on alert. The man even suggested and added words to add to the wire, and only charged Adam half the usual rate.

He had to admit that the women were right that Millie and Tate were better protected in town. Now Tate openly called him and Millie, "Unca Adam and Auntie Illie". Someone was always with the two of them when they walked around town. Millie's baking business swelled because people wanted her to bake for them, and then stayed at the house and visited while she made and baked their items.

If only they would hear from Millie's sister or father. Another week had passed without a letter or wire, causing Adam to worry that something else had happened that he and Millie didn't know about.

Adam heard the back door of the church open and close, but didn't think anything about it. Someone was really late and a guilty conscience made them come anyway, or more likely a child sneaking back in after going around back of the church to use one of the outhouses.

Tate had been sucking his thumb, lazily lying against Millie's shoulder, looking back at the children in the congregation. He suddenly jerked down, terror in his eyes as he punched Millie hard in the chest. She caught his fisted hand, and then looked into his eyes. Millie took a deep breath, quietly passed a hunched up Tate down the pew to Hilda. *What was going on?* Millie very slowly turned her head, carefully scanning the back of the church, and then slowly turned her head back. Adam started to lean over to ask Millie what was wrong because he could feel her trembling against his shoulder—when she leaned against his mother and whispered, "The wasp is here!"

Just like that his mother jumped up in the air, wildly waving her arms above her head shouting "There's a wasp in here!" Every woman in church immediately jumped up, screaming similar things about wasps, while pushing out of the pews and literally all swarming to the back of the church. The men and children were ducking down—as was the preacher—looking for a swarm of wasps in the air while the women ran to the back, down the center and side aisles.

Adam didn't know what to think or do as he watched the chaos erupt around him. His mother grabbed his coat collar, pulling him down so she could yell in his ear above the screams of the women. "Curtis Robbins is in the back of the church in a brown coat. Get him over to the jailhouse, now!"

"No! Where's Millie and Tate?" His mother pointed down to show Millie under the pew, with Hilda's arms covering Tate's body.

"The plan to protect them is in place, Adam. Do your part as marshal and get him away from the church and any view of the roads going south."

Adam pushed his way through the parishioners until he found a man surrounded by a tight ring of women. They were no longer swatting at imaginary wasps, but had their hands in their reticules... *Were they pointing hidden derringers at the man!?*

Good golly! Why had he ever thought that the town's women couldn't protect Millie and Tate? He needed to deputize women instead of men the next time he needed to form a posse.

Trying to politely nod at the sneering man, Adam said "Sir, I'm Marshal Wilerson and I believe you disturbed the peace by letting a swarm of wasps into the church service. Please come with me down to the jailhouse so we can discuss this matter."

"Hel..." Before Robbins got out the cuss word, one of the ladies yelled "Wasp!" and slapped at the insect that had mysteriously landed on the man's head.

"I suggest we move out of the church so the service can resume, sir."

"All right. I need you to press charges against a person who has kidnapped my son anyway, so let's get out of this den of....wasp slappers."

Adam wanted to slap this man's head with the butt of his gun, but he reminded himself that he, as the town marshal, was required to uphold the law of the state of Kansas. But right now he wanted to do the opposite thing that might be required of him.

He walked confidently beside the man, also wearing a badge, directing him to the jailhouse. Adam noticed other men walking slightly behind them, forming a back line of defense. "Please come in and have a seat, sir. "What's your name and business in my town?" Adam asked as business-like as possible.

The man held out his hand and Adam gave it a firm shake, wanting to crush the man while he had the chance, but refrained.

"I'm St. Louis city deputy marshal, Curtis Robbins. I wired you a couple of weeks ago about a woman and child, and you wired back that they were here. I..."

Robbins stopped talking when Jacob, Dagmar, Isaac Connely and his nephew Marcus Brenner filed in and shut the office door. "Why are these other men here for this private conversation?"

"These are my deputies, Robbins, so you may continue."

"You need four deputies to handle problems in this little squatter town?"

"Yes, we have our share of problems with the herds and cowboys that swarm around nearby Ellsworth this time of year, but they are also the reason we have no problems in Clear Creek.

"So why are you here, Robbins?" Adam refused to call him by his title because of the terror he caused Tate.

The man grinded his jaw side to side, like he was trying to contain his temper. "A Miss Millie Donavon stole my son Tate from my home three weeks ago, and I came to haul...ah, get him back, and to arrest Miss Donavon."

Adam closed his eyes to think. This man clearly knew his rights, but not as an abusive father. He needed the man to talk and hang the noose around his own neck with some slip of the tongue. "Did you know Miss Donovan? Why would she take your son?"

"I know they are here. So let me have them and I'll be on my way."

"I'm not even sure you are who you say you are, sir. You're in *my* town now, so you need to answer *me*." Adam glanced back at the four men standing against the wall with their arms folded against their chests. Dagmar was doing a very good impression of a mean, towering Viking. "Things are sometimes done a little differently in our 'squatter' towns versus your big cities." Adam tried not to smile when Robbins slightly squirmed in his seat.

"State your case. You've interrupted our Sunday service *and* my appetite for the fried chicken special I was planning to eat at the café afterwards."

Robbins cleared his throat. "Miss Donovan is my wife's sister and she didn't have my permission to take my son from my home."

"She had her sister's permission though," Adam asked, but more or less saying it as a statement.

Adam loved to see the man's skin color turn pinker. He wanted Robbins to take a swing at him, so he could swing back. "She…my wife…was giving birth to our baby so she wasn't in any shape to give consent."

"Congratulations on the new baby. Was it a boy or a girl?"

The man's stare said it all. He didn't know. Did he even know where his wife and baby were right now?

"Mister, why are you here when you should be home taking care of your wife and your new baby? I'm sure the boy's aunt is giving her sister time to recuperate from childbirth without having to take care of a busy toddler. Are you prepared to take care of him on the train ride home, and while your wife is taking care of an infant?"

"Cut the bull and the questions, Marshal. You know I have rights to that boy, and you and your silly townspeople need to hand him and his conniving aunt over to me."

"Why are you so desperate to get him back? Do you love you son—or need him for your punching bag?"

Robbins pulled a folded paper out of his pocket and slapped it on Adam's desk. "Here's the official warrant for the arrest of Miss Donavon…for the murder of my wife, Darcie Robbins. She's been feeding *you* a bunch of bull, Marshal Wilerson. She killed my wife, and then stole my child."

Chills ran up Adam's spine when he unfolded the paper and read the print. This was indeed a warrant for Millie's arrest. He had no choice but to turn her and Tate over to this man.

"Jacob, go over to the church and get them."

CHAPTER 12

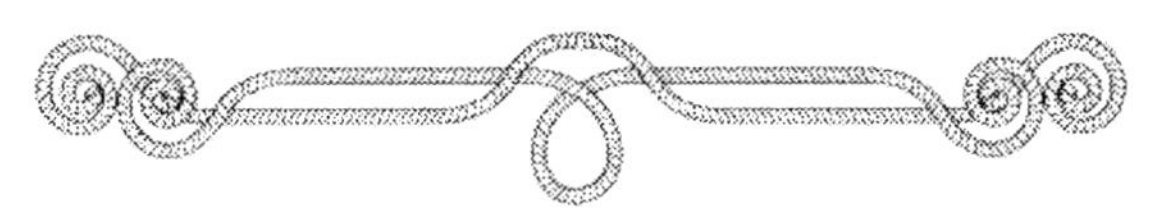

Millie was beyond scared and on to livid when Jacob came over to the church and explained what had happened at the jail. She wasn't worried about herself, but Tate. Was her sister really dead—or still hiding somewhere and Curtis was trying to flush Darcie out by bringing Millie and Tate back to St. Louis? She strongly suspected the latter and was determined to prove it. She was ready to shoot, both barrels of questions and red temper by the time she swung open the jail door, knocking the door knob straight into Dagmar's…thigh since he was so tall.

"I want to see that warrant, Marshal Wilerson." Millie thrust her hand out, ignoring Curtis getting up from his chair.

"You're under arrest, Millie Donovan for the murder of…"

"Oh, shut up Curtis. I'm reading."

Robbins started to grab her arm, but thought better of it when five men took a step closer.

"Marshal Wilerson, have you checked with the St. Louis Police Department to be sure this is on their records, and not a forged document?"

Adam didn't get a chance to answer before Curtis quickly interjected, "He doesn't need to wire the department because *it is real*."

"What was the cause of death then?"

"Uh, blunt force of an object."

"Where did it happen?"

"At home."

"Were there any witnesses?"

"No."

"Wasn't there someone helping her with your infant son?"

"No."

"Then how do you know it was me?"

"Uh, a neighbor saw you leave the house and notified me."

"Where were you when this happened, and why weren't you there helping take care of your new son?"

"I had things to do so I had to leave for a while."

Millie paused with her rapid questions, giving Curtis time to think he had proved his accusation. Then she turned on the tears…

"Did you bury her in her favorite blue dress?" she whispered, shocking all six men with her turn of questions.

"Uh..."

"Were there many friends and neighbors at the wake at your home?"

"Uh..."

"Was it Father Devin or Father Tim who conducted the ceremony at the Cathedral?"

"Uh, Father Tim."

"Marshal Wilerson, be sure to wire to the Cathedral of St. Louis office for the record of Darcie's service and internment, besides the police department. There would also be a notice in the newspaper of her death, because I'm sure Curtis would have done everything proper for his beloved wife."

Curtis was losing traction and she wanted to finish nailing his case shut. "How did my father handle his daughter's death?"

He stared at Millie, knowing he didn't have a case against her, because no way would Ennis Donovan miss his daughter's funeral. Curtis lunged at Millie, getting both hands around her neck and getting one hard squeeze in, making Millie drop to her knees before the men wrestled Curtis to the floor.

"Millie..." Adam tried to help Millie off the floor, but she slapped his hand away and crawled up to Curtis's face which was smashed against the wooden floor.

"I helped deliver your baby *girl* into the world after you kicked Darcie out of your bedroom, and *her* name is Amelia Moran."

Curtis' shocked look pleased Millie, because it meant that he hadn't found Darcie. "So, you haven't seen that child yet…and you never will. And you have no right to Tate either, because I have a signed and notarized paper stating that *I* am Tate's guardian now. This was filled out when Darcie filed her divorce papers against you…which I bet you've already been served. You thought you could kidnap us, and get Darcie to drop the divorce and come back to you to continue as your punching bag."

Millie gathered up her skirt to stand and straightened her shoulders. She looked at Curtis first, and then Adam. "Never, *ever*, under estimate a policeman's daughter." She spun on her heel to march out of there before she really blew her curls, but she turned back for one shout, "…or any angry woman for that matter."

CHAPTER 13

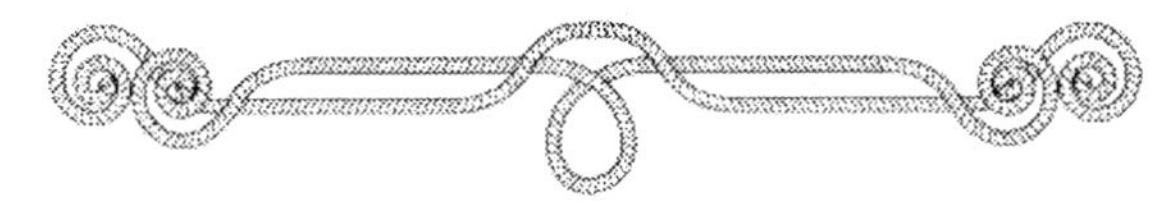

Adam sat at his desk, looking at the empty cell that had just been vacated. It had been a rough week and he was glad it was over. He couldn't stand looking at the man who hurt Tate and Millie's sister. Adam knew it was mean and spiteful, but Robbins got very, very small portions in the meals Adam shoved through the cell bars. Once the food slid off the plate onto the floor and wasn't replaced. Adam locked the jail up and spent most of the week outside so he could get away from the rants of the lunatic.

Sunday afternoon had been spent wiring the St. Louis police station, and waiting for a wire reply. As it turned out, there was a warrant out for Curtis, for beating up another policeman to the point the officer died, but not before telling the chief of police who had done it to him.

Adam was told to keep Robbins in the Clear Creek jail until he was picked up by authorities. There was a U.S. Marshal coming through on a train from Denver, so he would transport Robbins back to St. Louis.

The wires to the Cathedral and the St. Louis newspaper were answered on Monday, with no knowledge of the deaths of Darcie or her baby. That could be good or bad news. Robbins swore he didn't know where they were of course, so they were either hiding or buried in a shallow grave somewhere. Adam shuddered, thinking of a woman looking like Millie going through…either situation.

The police checked on the Robbins's neighbor where Millie had left Darcie, but her house was empty. Adam even wired back to the Chicago police, trying to send a message to Mr. Donovan that Robbins was arrested, but that Darcie and her baby hadn't been found yet.

And Adam came home Sunday evening to an empty house. There was no evidence of the woman and child who had been living in his home. Millie even took the tins of sugar and cookies with her, because he looked, needing a cookie, even if Millie wasn't there to give him a Baker's Kiss.

Henry filled him in on the outside activity while they were in the jail that afternoon. Hilda, on Nutcracker, had high-tailed it out of town with Tate in the saddle in front of her as soon as the jailhouse door was shut when he and Robbins went to talk.

Cate, Sarah and Rania arrived at his house shortly after that in a wagon, and had the wagon full and ready to leave when Millie stormed out of the jailhouse and boarded the wagon, never stepping a foot in his house.

And no one had breathed a word of where Millie and Tate were now. The men in town were clueless and the women were ignoring him. He had tried his best to protect Millie and Tate, but it seems like the female population in town thought otherwise. He was back to eating all his meals at the café and darn if something wasn't burned on his plate every meal. It didn't matter if it was chicken or pie, Edna Clancy had it out for him. Of course it didn't help that he'd been spoiled on Millie's cooking and baking.

Out of habit he pulled Millie's letters out of the desk drawer. The paper edges were getting worn from him reading each one and putting them back into the envelopes so much. Why was he punishing himself by doing this? Because he loved Millie, and truly missed seeing her in his home. No, not his home, it should be their home.

The situation with Robbins was settled and time for him to get Millie home, only he was ready for her to be his bride, not his housekeeper. He eyed the letters on his desk, thinking of a way to propose.

Adam looked up as the door opened, pleased to finally see his mother again. She had been avoiding him, too.

"Hello, Ma. Robbins was picked up an hour ago, so it's safe for Millie and Tate to come back to town now."

"I'm glad to hear that. Any word on Millie's sister or baby?"

Adam blew out a breath and shook his head. "I've wired everywhere I could think of to find a clue of their whereabouts, plus Chicago again trying to find her father." He wiped his hand across his face in frustration. "The three of them have disappeared, either trying to hide, or Robbins got to them first and isn't admitting what he did."

Cate nodded in agreement. “It’s very possible we’ll never know what happened to them. Then Millie really will be raising Tate.”

“I assume you know where they are, Ma?” Adam asked his mother. She just shrugged her shoulders at his statement. Adam asked Jacob two days ago if Millie and Tate were at any of their places out in the country, but he said no. The women had taken them someplace else.

“I’ve been thinking about writing for a mail-order bride, Ma,” Adam said as he ran his finger on the edge of the paper he had been reading…again. “When I read Millie’s letters, I was intrigued by getting to know a person by their words and how they wrote their thoughts out. It made me…listen to the person talking without being distracted by outside things.”

“And how are you going to advertise for this mail-order bride?”

“There’s only one person I’d like to apply for the position, and I’m hoping that a special ‘mail-carrier’ can get it to her.” Adam held his breath, waiting for his mother’s reaction. He had disappointed her so badly with the whole situation until now.

“You write the letter and I’ll see if delivery can be arranged,” his mother said with a slight smile on her face. “Shall I do a little shopping and come back here before I leave for the ranch?”

“Yes, please. I’d appreciate your help.” Adam relished the pat his mother gave him on the arm. But then she turned and walked out the door without another word. He sighed, knowing he needed to get back in the good graces of several women.

Adam pulled a piece of paper from his desk and then took the cap off his ink jar. He stared at the paper, wishing the jumbled words in his head could flow onto the paper without all the interference that was plaguing his mind. He took a deep breath and starting writing his thoughts and wishes down to the woman he loved.

***

He waved the piece of stationery to dry the ink, then folded and stuffed it in an envelope before he changed his mind. Adam didn't know what he would do if Millie didn't respond back. He had found his true love, but had blown his first chance with her. Adam wiped his face, and then folded his hands in prayer, wishing for a second chance. *Please let her write back, and with a positive answer.*

Adam looked up when the door opened.

"You weren't gone very long, Ma."

"Actually I just walked a few blocks to give you time to write your letter. Ready for your letter to be delivered?"

"Are you sure I can't deliver it in person?"

"Let Millie make the first move, Adam. It's her choice if she wants to marry you, or even stay in Kansas. Please don't push her."

"Do I have a choice?" he asked. His mother shrugged her shoulders again, but at least she had a smile on her face.

***

Millie sat on the porch of the Cross C Ranch house, staring at the vast open landscape that lay before the house. The grass rolled over one hill, disappearing in a valley then rolled up into view again. And not a tree in sight...

She had grown to respect and admire the Kansas prairie, knowing it can be dangerous due to weather or circumstances, but at least you usually "saw trouble coming" as Adam once told her.

She missed the house in town with a deep passion that surprised her. It had become home, and she missed the simple life of Clear Creek, the townspeople—good and bad who made up the character of the town. You couldn't blend into the background like Chicago, but here people cared, honestly and truly *cared.*

Millie looked around the ranch yard to find Tate down by the corrals with Isaac. Although Isaac wasn't much over forty, his silver hair made Tate think of the man as a grandfather figure, and Tate adored him. The boy had grown in weight, height and self-esteem since fleeing St. Louis. She had done the right thing for her sister's child. And without any word from her sister, Millie had accepted the fact that she was indeed Tate's guardian and would be raising him by herself.

Stop playing the past over and over in your mind, Millie. Think ahead.

But what was ahead? Millie didn't know if Adam would want her back in town after her outburst in the jailhouse. She was mad when Adam didn't question Curtis's plot right away and her temper had flared red hot when she marched in on the men. Millie still couldn't believe Adam thought that was a real warrant for her arrest, but then she hadn't talked to him since then. Maybe he was dealing with it in his own way when she butted in. But oh it felt good to speak her mind to Curtis while his face was smashed to the floor. She could have kicked a pointed boot toe up his nose too, but then she'd be no better than he was, beating on a person.

Should she stay on the Cross C Ranch as Isaac's housekeeper? The ranch's housekeeper recently moved away, so Millie had taken over her duties. It was a nice home, but only Isaac and Marcus to keep house for so she had time to play with Tate, and watch the quiet life of the ranch from this porch. But Isaac was good friends with the Wilersons, so it would be hard to be around Adam if he and she weren't together.

Tate would do wonderful here, but he'd need to go to school in a few years, and she still wanted to marry and have a family too. Should she move on to a bigger city to find a job, or stay here, looking at the view and wishing for more?

Millie heard Tate's excited squeal before noticing the buggy coming up the drive. She stepped off the porch and shaded her eyes to see who their visitor was. Any company would be welcome on this quiet afternoon.

She recognized the horse, and then the driver as the buggy pulled to a stop beside Isaac and Tate. As soon as Cate stepped down to the ground, Tate launched himself at her. He had grown so attached to Cate, and all of the Wilersons.

Millie hadn't talked to Cate's family since they moved her and Tate out to the Cross C.

Because Isaac had been in the office with Adam last Sunday, he told her what had happened after Millie left. She wasn't surprised that Curtis, with his temper, was wanted for a murder and was in the Clear Creek jail waiting for transportation back to St. Louis.

Hopefully, Cate was coming out with more news now.

Tate jumped up and down while holding Cate's hand and walking towards the house. Millie took a deep breath, dreading the meeting, but needing to know if Adam had found her sister yet. And she wanted to know how Adam was doing. Was he missing her and Tate, or glad they were gone from his house? Had he and Cate even talked?

"Millie, it's so good to see you," Cate said as she opened her arms and pulled Millie into a tender hug. "How have you been?"

"Okay. Adjusting to this quiet place. Tate loves it here…Any news about Darcie?"

"I've been in to see Adam this afternoon and Robbins is now in the custody of a U.S. Marshal and on his way to St. Louis. Unfortunately, as many places as Adam has wired looking for your sister and her baby, he doesn't have any news yet. They seem to have vanished at the moment."

Cate hesitated, then added. "Adam's also been looking for your father. Back when you wrote to your father, Adam sent a wire to the Chicago Police trying to tell him of the problems going on here for you, and for your sister in St. Louis."

"He never told me that, Cate."

"He didn't want you to think he was interfering with your family, but he was trying to help you even back then. More wires to Chicago since still haven't located your father. Adam's gotten wires stating that your father left his job and the police station doesn't know where he went." Cate paused in thought. "I wonder if your father got the first wire from Adam, then took off for St. Louis?"

"Surely he'd let me know if he'd found Darcie though?"

Cate patted her arm. "We'll just keep praying that we'll hear soon.

"Well, do you and Tate like it out here? I've always loved the view from this porch."

"I must admit I miss the noises in town, but Tate enjoys the animals and the attention Isaac and Marcus gives him. I'm…toying with the idea of moving on to Denver though, once I've gained funds to do so."

Cate pulled a letter out of her reticule, tapped it against her gloved hand a few times before holding it out to Millie. "Here's an opportunity you might want to consider first. If you want to answer back, let me know and I'll pass the message on to the writer.

"How about this young man and me go into the kitchen and see what we can find for drinks and treats?" Cate looked down at Tate when she sweetly talked. "I know my way around Isaac's kitchen so you can read your letter in peace while Tate and I play host and hostess. Isaac will be in for coffee when he's done taking care of my horse."

Millie looked at the envelope, recognizing Adam's big scrawl on the front panel. It was addressed to "A Mail-order Bride". That caught her curiosity enough to open the envelope and pull out the letter. Her hands trembled with the thought that Adam was writing for a bride, and what, needed her help in finding one?

Dear Ma'am,

I'm looking for a mail-order bride with certain qualifications and wondering if you'd like to apply.

I want a beautiful woman, with an Irish lilt in her voice. It would be an extra asset if she had long red curly hair and a fiery temperament to match it.

There would be a wonderful extended family and group of friends who would be included with the groom, including a very helpful a mother-in-law and sisters-in-law.

I'd appreciate a ready-made family and would love to have a little boy be a part of our marriage ceremony. More children in the future would make our family complete.

She needs to accept the fact that she would live in a very small town with lots of wide-open prairie around it. A nice, two-story house, with a fenced yard and chicken house would be her home. Chickens and a cat come with the place—along with two baby-sitters just a block away.

The only thing I need to caution her about is that the groom is the town marshal, and can be in danger as part of his job. He tries his best to do the right thing by the law, and recently learned he must think with his heart, besides his head, in certain cases.

The man in question has, in the past, had a lapse in judgment that hurt someone he very much loved, but he plans not to do that again—if there is any way he can avoid it.

If you are interested in this particular groom and conditions, could you please write back to me in care of Cate Wilerson, or whoever delivers this letter?

With deep admiration and love,

Adam Wilerson

P.S. Millie, will you marry me, please? I love you and Tate with all my heart.

Drops of moisture fell on the letter and smeared a word as Millie read the last line. She quickly wiped her eyes, not wanting to destroy a word on this precious letter.

Now what will she do? She could accept this proposal, or move on to Denver. Which would be best for her, and Tate? Could she and Adam have a good life together, or would his job cause her to be an early widow with more children to support?

Millie wiped her eyes again as Tate burst open the screen door of the house. "Tate, please go see what's keeping Isaac while I talk to your aunt. Okay?"

"'Kay, Gamma."

Cate eased down in a chair by Millie, but keeping her eye on Tate as he toddled across the yard toward the barn. "I think he's grown since I last saw him four days ago. This sunshine and fresh air has been good for him." Then she turned to look at Millie, her smile fading, replaced by a serious inquiry.

"I don't know what Adam wrote, but he asked that this letter be delivered to you. No one has told him where you are, so it's your decision to write back to him or not."

Millie sighed as she met Cate's eyes. "He wrote a sweet proposal asking for a mail-order bride, but he spelled out that the person would have to put up with being married to a lawman. It made me think of my parents' marriage, and I can't decide if I want that for myself or Tate."

"Tell me how your father's job affected your parents' marriage."

"Whenever Pa walked out the door, we knew that he might not come back. Danger could snatch his life at any time."

"How did your mother handle the worry?"

Millie thought back to her early childhood. How did her mother handle it? She smiled now at the memory. "Actually she gave him a kiss before he walked out the door each morning and said, 'May the good saints protect you and bless you today.' She said that *every* morning until…*she* died."

"Life is constant—and changing," Cate mused. "We can never guess what will happen in a day. We will all face danger, and finally death, be it from an accident, disease or old age."

Cate was silent for several minutes, staring across the distant grass in thought. "I never thought of my husband dying from cancer at such a young age. We planned to live to a ripe old age together—with rheumatism, hard hearing and a houseful of visiting great grandchildren.

"I wasn't prepared for his departure, but yet I had time to adjust because of his slow death. It would have been far worse if his life was cut short instantly by a bullet, or a mad bull in our pasture."

"So how did you cope, Cate? I'm not positive I can take the chance of loving Adam, only to lose him in a gunfight down the street."

"The question is—do you want to love him while you can—or walk away now? Do you think you'd always wish you had those years together—be it one or fifty—or you'd be happier marrying someone else being a railroad worker or a tailor? Just remember that anyone could fall off a ladder or be killed in some fashion you never thought of. Experience has already told you 'that's life' hasn't it?"

Yes, that was so true. And try as she might, Millie could only see Adam as her husband, gun strapped around his waist as always.

Then Cate added, "As Adam's mother, I want you to be sure you'll love him as he is. My son deserves love and respect because he is a good man. Even as a boy, he had the 'what's right is right, and what's wrong is wrong' attitude, and that's what makes him a passionate lawman. A wife can't and shouldn't change him, just as a husband probably couldn't change a red-haired woman's temper," Cate added with a pointed finger and a crooked smile.

"Oh so true, Cate. 'Me Irish roots run deep' as my mother always said, and it continues through my blood, and Tate's too when he gets in one of his stubborn moods."

Millie looked across the yard again and sighed. “Tate is happy here in Clear Creek. I’d hate to pull him away from the new family he’s formed around him.”

“But how about you? What do you want? What’s the first thing that pops into your mind?”

“I want to be with Adam *and* his family…” Millie grinned.

CHAPTER 14

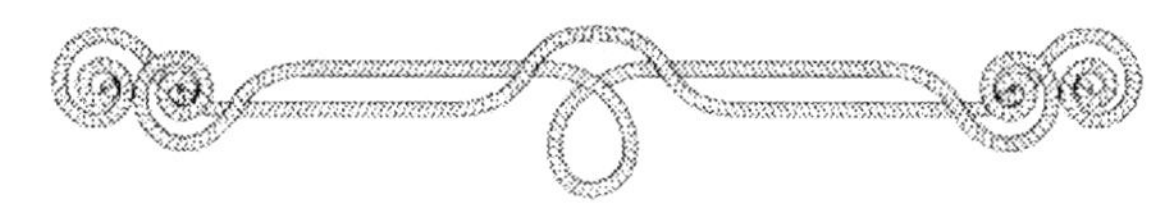

Adam's eyes lit up when he saw his mother had an envelope in her hand. Millie had written back! He snatched it from her and tore open the envelope before his mother had a chance to sit down in the office chair.

Dear Sir,

I have received your letter and will accept being your mail-order bride—if you will agree to my conditions also.

First, I want us to live by this old Irish proverb. "Don't walk in front of me, I may not follow. Don't walk behind me, I may not lead. Walk beside me and just be my friend." We will be equal partners and make important decisions together for our family.

Also:

You will try to be as safe as possible in your job, and will take the suggestions of a policeman's daughter if they are offered, because she does have experience with this kind of work.

You will help raise my nephew as your own son, along with as many children as the good Lord gives us.

You will allow our family to get a medium-sized dog (preferably one that doesn't yap all the time).

You will always have a one-pound tin of powdered sugar in our bedroom for "Baker's Kisses".

If you are interested in this particular bride and conditions, please be waiting for me at the altar this Sunday after church, for our marriage ceremony.

With love,

Millie Donovan

"*She said 'Yes'!* I'm getting married on Sunday, Ma!"

***

Millie stood with Adam on her right and Sarah on her left at the front of the church, trying not to visibly shake as the preacher started their wedding ceremony. She was outfitted in a beautiful dark blue silk dress with a high bustle in the back. It was trimmed with white lace on the collar and wrists and was the most gorgeous dress she had ever worn. A fashionable hat, made from the same fabric and lace crowned her curly red hair.

As soon as her new sisters-in-law heard she was joining the family on Sunday, they sprang into action. Cate insisted Millie and Tate spend Saturday night at the Wilerson ranch before the ceremony. Rania moved Millie's and Tate's belongings back to

Adam's house, except what she and Tate needed overnight. Meanwhile Sarah drove Millie out to the Bar E home for Cora's surprise contribution. The women went through Cora's vast wardrobe to find the perfect Boston-made gown for Millie to wear for her wedding. Irish brides wore blue for their weddings so Millie wanted to go with a blue theme for her special day. Cora even insisted Millie keep the dress and hat as her wedding gift.

Millie felt so blessed standing in front of the church with the Wilersons surrounding her and Tate with love, understanding—and patience. There was no doubt in Millie's mind that she was supposed to be Adam's wife, so she was marrying a marshal today. She was prepared for the good and the bad that could happen in their future, because she'd have the support of his family and town if worse came to worst.

Her only regret was not having her Irish family here today, but Kaitlyn Reagan tried her best to fill that gap. Trying to work in Irish traditions, Kaitlyn wrapped blue ribbon around a new horseshoe for Millie to carry with her flower nosegay. The horseshoe, open end up, would be nailed above their front door for good luck after the ceremony.

Adam probably wondered about the short piece of rope that was draped across the altar, but it would be used during the ceremony to wrap around their clasped hands to symbolize their "tying the knot", or their agreement to spend their lives together.

Cate had asked Millie to take off Sam's ring she had been wearing. She wasn't sure what Adam had in mind for a ring, but she'd soon find out.

Millie turned her attention to Pastor Reagan when he cleared his throat and said, "Dearly Beloved, we are gathered here today in the sight of God and angels, and the presence of friends and loved ones, to celebrate one of life's greatest moments, to unite Adam and Millie in holy matrimony".

Millie heard the back door of the church quietly open, then an infant's soft cry. She tuned out the sounds and turned her attention back to Pastor Reagan.

"If there be anyone who has cause why this couple should not be united in marriage, they must speak now or forever hold their peace."

"I do," boomed a man's voice in the back of the church. "We need to start over. I have the right to walk me daughter down the aisle first."

"Da?" Millie turned when she thought she heard her father's voice. Then the whole congregation turned to see a large man with a ruddy complexion and orange-red hair beaming at this daughter, and a thin young woman who matched Millie in looks.

"Momma?" Tate, being held by Sarah, who was standing beside Millie, squirmed down to the floor when he saw his mother in the back of the church.

"Wasp?" The elderly Mrs. Benson yelled, slowly pulling herself up by the seat back in front of her as Tate streaked by her pew.

***

They began the service again, with her father walking her down the aisle and Darcie following them carrying Tate. Darcie's neighbor Flora Davis, holding baby Amelia, was seated in the front row with a beaming Kaitlyn Reagan.

Millie joyously stated her vows in a clear voice, knowing she would be happy with Adam, living in their little prairie town. The only thing that surprised her was when Adam slipped her wedding band on her finger and whispered, "Let love and friendship reign". Kaitlyn had helped Adam pick out a ring that had a heart in the design, to symbolize the Irish Claddagh ring. The design of the traditional ring has three key elements: a heart for love, a pair of hands for friendship, and a crown for loyalty, and Adam's simple statement was the motto of the ring's symbol. Millie believed the wedding couldn't have been better if they had weeks to plan it.

Now the congregation had moved outside to set up the picnic reception, and Millie was introducing her family to the Wilersons.

Millie never would have guessed when she answered Sam's letter to be his mail-order bride, that she would be marrying his friend instead, and gaining an extended network of family and friends in the bargain.

And now her immediate family would fill Adam's and her house to capacity, but she knew Adam welcomed them with open arms, just like the rest of the Wilersons and Hamners. The luck of the Irish delivered them all safely to their new home in this little Kansas town.

"Saint Catherine, I want you to meet Saint Flora," Millie grinned with pleasure. Both women laughed but with questions on their faces. "Cate, you were my 'saint' helping me here in Clear Creek, while Flora was Darcie's in St. Louis.

"Every morning, when our father left the house to go to work, our mother said, 'May the good saints protect you and bless you today.' When my sister and I were down on our luck, you ladies came to our rescue. We can't thank you enough for your protection and guidance."

"And Darcie, these are my new sisters, Sarah, Rania, her twin Hilda, and our special friend, Cora who gave me this gorgeous gown..." Millie stopped talking and looked down when she felt a tug on her skirt.

"Auntie Illie, Unca Adam needs a kiss," Tate solemnly stated. Millie felt her face flush with embarrassment, and excitement.

"Oh, does he have a boo-boo that needs a Baker's Kiss?" Millie asked Tate, while watching Adam sneak up behind her to wrap his arms around her waist. Darcie and Flora looked clueless, but the other women chuckled, knowing how Millie took care of Tate's little mishaps and worries.

"Where are the tins of magic sugar and cookies?" Millie asked, still talking to Tate. She melted in Adam's arms though when her whispered in her ear, "Up in our bedroom..."

Yes, Millie married a marshal—but she was sure with her luck—they would have a long life together, filled with lots of love and kisses.

EPILOGUE

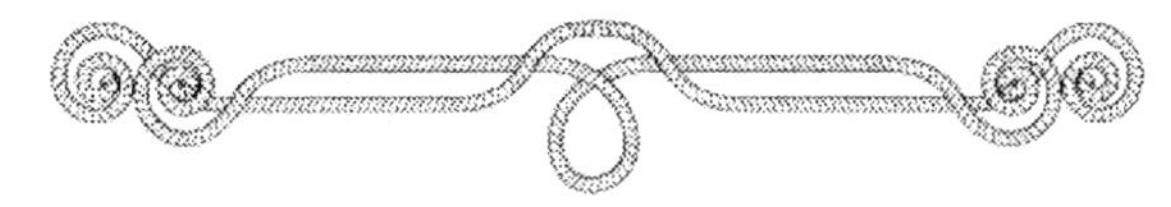

A week later...

Adam read the first of two wires that had just been delivered to him at the jailhouse. The wire from St. Louis stated that Curtis Robbins had been sentenced to hang for the murder of a fellow lawman. Adam hated that a life would be taken, but was relieved that his wife and her family were finally free of the man.

The second wire made him chuckle. His brother Noah was boarding the train in Denver today and would arrive home later this week. Adam couldn't wait for Noah's reaction when he found out his unfinished homestead claim had been bought and taken over by a woman—and a little yapping dog...

Dear Readers: I hope you're enjoying the **Brides with Grit** series, and meeting the Wilerson and Hamner families.

My goal for this series is to honor the strong women who lived on the Kansas prairie during the frontier years. The characters and their stories were fabricated in my mind after viewing photos of real couples in my great grandparent's photo album. These 1800s photos were used for the book covers too.

The series setting is based on the famous old cowtown of Ellsworth, Kansas during its cattle drive days. The town of Clear Creek though, is fictional, based on the many little towns that sprang up as the railroad was built across Kansas.

This particular area is now the current Kanopolis State Park in central Kansas. Being local to where I live, I've hiked the park's hiking trails, where it's easy to visualize what the area looked like in 1873—because it remains the same now—as then.

Although not all of the **Brides with Grit** titles are published yet as of this book's printing, please look for the following titles on Amazon.com to find out when they are available.

Rania Ropes a Rancher (Rania and Jacob)

Millie Marries a Marshal (Millie and Adam)

Hilda Hogties a Horseman (Hilda and Noah)

Cora Captures a Cowboy (Cora and Dagmar)

Sarah Snares a Soldier (Sarah and Marcus)

Cate Corrals a Cattleman (Cate and Isaac)

Darcie Desires a Drover (Darcie and Reuben)

Tina Tracks a Trail Boss (Tina and Leif)

Rania Ropes a Rancher

A Historical Western Romance

Brides with Grit Series, Book 1

Rania Hamner and her family emigrated from Sweden fourteen years ago to work on a Texas ranch, working cattle and herding them up the Chisholm Trail. Something in her life on the trail caused her to doubt her worth, and her ability to trust a man enough to become his wife. Once the family buys a homestead in Kansas, she meets a rancher who begins to make her believe she can trust and fall in love after all.

Rancher Jacob Wilerson noticed Rania last year when she rode drag behind a herd of longhorns—right down Main Street of Ellsworth, Kansas. He's been waiting for her family to return this spring with another Texas herd to the booming cowtown, because he hopes to rope her into staying permanently on his ranch—the way she had already roped his heart.

When Rania's past attacks with new danger, she decides to fight for all she's worth because she realizes she wants to be with Jacob forever.

When Jacob realizes Rania is in danger, he rushes to save her, whether or not she still loves him, hoping to rope Rania—his heart—once more, as she has roped his.

Historical Fiction Books by Linda K. Hubalek

Trail of Thread

A Woman's Westward Journey, Historical Letters 1854-1855

Trail of Thread Series, Book 1

Taste the dust of the road and feel the wind in your face as you travel with a Kentucky family by wagon train to the new territory of Kansas in 1854.

Find out what it was like for the thousands of families who made the cross-country journey into the unknown.

In this first book of the *Trail of Thread* series; in the form of letters she wrote on the journey, Deborah Pieratt describes the scenery, the everyday events on the trail, and the task of taking care of her family. Stories of humor and despair, along with her ongoing remarks about camping, cooking, and quilting on the wagon trail make you feel as if you pulled up stakes and are traveling with the Pieratt's, too.

But hints of the brewing trouble ahead plagued them along the way as people questions their motive for settling in the new territory. If they are from the South, why don't they have slaves with them? Would the Pieratt's vote for or against legal slavery in the new state? Though Deborah does not realize it, her letters show how this trip affected her family for generations to come.

This series is based on author Linda K. Hubalek's ancestors that traveled from Kentucky to Kansas in 1854.

Thimble of Soil

A Woman's Quest for Land, Historical Letters 1854-1860

Trail of Thread Series, Book 2

Experience the terror of the fighting and the determination to endure as you stake a claim alongside the women caught in the bloody conflicts of Kansas in the 1850's.

Follow the widowed Margaret Ralston Kennedy (a relative of the author) in this second book of the *Trail of Thread* series, as she travels with eight of her thirteen children from Ohio to the Territory of Kansas in 1855.

Thousands of Americans headed west in the decade before the Civil War, but those who settled in Kansas suffered through frequent clashes between proslavery and free-state fractions that gripped the territory.

Told through her letters, *Thimble of Soil* describes the prevalent hardships and infrequent joys experienced by the hardy pioneer women of Kansas, who struggled to protect their families from terrorist raids while building new homes and new lives on the vast unbroken prairie.

Margaret was dedicated to the cause of the North, and while the male members of her family were away fighting for a free state, she valiantly defended their homestead and held their families together through the savage years of Bleeding Kansas.

Stitch of Courage

A Woman's Fight of Freedom, Historical Letters 1861-1865

Trail of Thread Series, Book 3

Feel the uncertainty, doubt, and danger faced by the pioneer women as they defend their homes and pray for their men during the Civil War.

Stitch of Courage, the third book in the *Trail of Thread* series, tells the story of the orphaned Maggie Kennedy, who followed her brothers to Kansas in the late 1850s.

The niece of Margaret Ralston Kennedy, the main character in Hubalek's *Thimble of Soil* book, Maggie married the son of Deborah Pieratt, whose story was told in the Hubalek's *Trail of Thread* book.

In letters to her sister in Ohio, Maggie describes how the women of Kansas faced the demons of the Civil War, fighting bravely to protect their homes and families while never knowing from one day to the next whether their men were alive or dead on the faraway battlefield.

We think the Civil War took place in the South, but the Plains States endured their share of battles and tragedy. Not only did Kansas and Missouri experience a resurgence in the terrorist raids that plagued them in the years before the war, the Confederate Army tried several times to sweep across the Great Plains and capture the West.

Butter in the Well

A Scandinavian Woman's Tale of Life on the Prairie, 1868-1888

Butter in the Well Series, Book 1

Read the fictionalized account of Kajsa Svenson Runeberg, an emigrant wife who recounts, through her diary, how she and her family built up a farm on the unsettled Kansas prairie from 1868 to 1888.

This historical fiction is based on the actual Swedish woman who homesteaded the author's childhood home and is the first of the four-book *Butter in the Well* series.

"...could well be the most endearing 'first settler' account ever told. Once a reader starts the book, they are compelled to keep reading to see what will happen next on the isolated prairie homestead. Not to be missed! — *Capper's Family Bookstore*

Hubalek has skillfully blended fiction and historic fact to recreate the life of Swedish homestead, Kajsa Svensson Runeberg. A story of emigrant dreams and pioneer struggles, it is an altogether rewarding story and one that deserves to be told. — *Kansas State Historical Society*

Prairie Bloomin'

The Prairie Blossoms for an Immigrant's Daughter, 1889-1900

Butter in the Well Series, Book 2

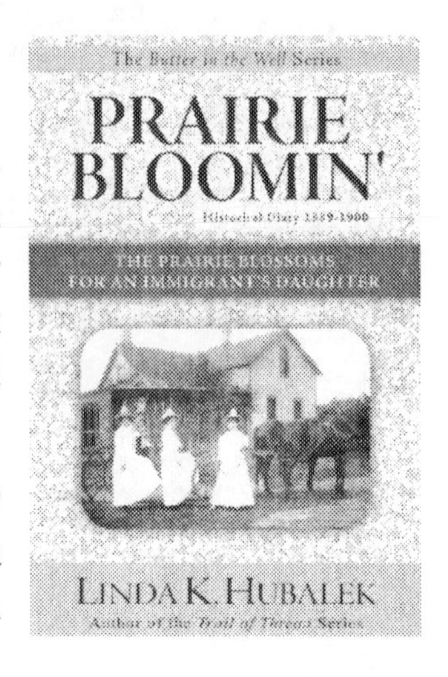

Popular Kansas author Linda K. Hubalek continues the story of a Swedish immigrant family featured in the *Butter in the Well* series with the second book *Prairie Bloomin'* (formerly titled *Prärieblomman*).

Prairie Bloomin' features the 1889 to 1900 diary of daughter Alma Swenson, as she grows up on the farm her parents homesteaded.

Even though born on the same farm in two different centuries, Prairie Bloomin's main character, Alma Swenson Runneberg, and the author shared uncanny similarities while growing up in the Smoky Valley region of central Kansas. Both the third child of their families, they lived in the same house, played in the same yard and worked the same acres until each married and moved off the farm.

"…is a tender and touching diary…Hubalek has succeeded in blowing life into both Alma and the fascinating times she lived through. Hubalek's books give Swedish-Americans a perspective of the past." *Anders Neumueller, Swedish Press, Vancouver, BC Canada*

Egg Gravy

Authentic Recipes from the Butter in the Well Series

Butter in the Well Series, Book 3

Faded recipes. We've all come across them from time to time in our lives, either handwritten by ourselves or by another person in our family, or as old yellowed newspaper clippings stuck in a cookbook of sorts.

While doing research for the *Butter in the Well* series, the author found old recipes and home remedies along with family and community histories.

These recipes had been handwritten in old ledger books, on scraps of paper, in the margins of old cookbooks and forever etched in the memories of those pioneer women's children that Linda Hubalek interviewed.

As a result, *Egg Gravy* is a collection of recipes the pioneer women used during their homesteading days. Most of the recipes can be traced back to the original women that homesteaded the real-life setting of *Butter in the Well.* Antique family photos add a personal feel to the cookbook.

From Green Pumpkin Pie, Caramel Ice Cream, and Smoked Pig Paunch to Christine's Fruit Cake, Apple Sauce Cake, and Rhubarb Marmalade, these are culinary samplings of a yesteryear that would grace any menu today. — *Midwest Book Review*

Looking Back

The Final Tale of Life on the Prairie, 1919

Butter in the Well Series, Book 4

The inevitable happens—time moves on and we grow older. Instead of our own little children surrounding us, grandchildren take their place.

Each new generation lives in a new age of technology, not realizing the changes the generations before theirs has seen-and improved for them.

The cycle of life has change the prairie also. Endless waves of tall native prairie grass have been reduced to uniform rows of grain crops. The curves of the river have shifted over the decades, eroded by both man and nature. The majestic prairie has been tamed over time.

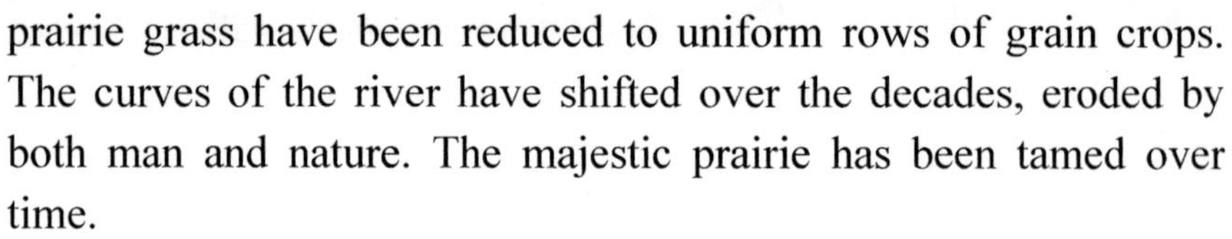

In this fourth book of the *Butter in the Well* series, Kajsa Svensson Runeberg, now age 75, looks back at the changes she has experienced on the farm she homesteaded 51 years ago. She reminisces about the past, resolves the present situation, and looks toward their future off the farm.

Don't miss this heart-rending touching finale!

Planting Dreams

A Swedish Immigrant's Journey to America, 1868-1869

Planting Dreams Series, Book 1

Can you imagine starting a journey to an unknown country in 1868, not knowing what the country would be like, where you would live, or how you would survive? Did you make the right decision to leave in the first place?

This first book in the *Planting Dreams* series portrays Swedish immigrant Charlotta Johnson (author Linda Hubalek's ancestor), as she ponders the decision to leave her homeland, travel to America, and worries about her family's future in a new country.

Each chapter is written as a thought-provoking story as the family travels to a new country to find a new life.

Why did this family leave? Drought scorched the farmland of Sweden and there was no harvest to feed families or livestock. Taxes were due and there was little money to pay them. But there were ships sailing to America, where the government gave land to anyone who wanted to claim a homestead.

Follow Charlotta and her family as they travel by ship and rail from Sweden, to their homestead on the open plains of Kansas.

Cultivating Hope

Homesteading on the Great Plains, 1869-1886

Planting Dreams Series, Book 2

Can you imagine being isolated in the middle of treeless grassland with only a dirt roof over your head? Having to feed your children with whatever wild plants or animals you could find living on the prairie?

Sweating to plow the sod, plant the seed, cultivate the crop—only to lose it all by a hailstorm right before you harvest it?

This second book in the *Planting Dreams* series portrays Swedish immigrant Charlotta Johnson as she and her husband build a farmstead on the Kansas prairie.

This family faced countless challenges as they homestead on America's Great Plains during the 1800s. Years of hard work develop the land and improve the quality of life for her family—but not with a price.

Readers compare Hubalek's books as a combination of Laura Ingalls Wilder's *Little House on the Prairie* books, *The Emigrants* series by Vilhelm Moberg, and a Willa Cather novel.

Harvesting Faith

Life on the Changing Prairie, 1886-1919

Planting Dreams Series, Book 3

Imagine surveying your farmstead on the last day of your life, reviewing the decades of joys, hardships, and changes that have taken place on the eighty acres you have called home for the past fifty years. Would you feel at peace or find remorse at the decisions that took place in your life?

This third book in the *Planting Dreams* series portrays Charlotta Johnson as she recalls the events that shaped her family's destiny. A mixture of fact and fiction, based on the author's family, this book reviews the events that shaped this Swedish immigrants family as her children reached adulthood and had families of their own.

Join Charlotta as she reminisces about the important places and events in her past as she bids farewell to her mortal life on the Kansas prairie.

ABOUT THE AUTHOR

Linda Hubalek majored in agriculture in college, and featured in *Country Woman Magazine* about her wildflower business when her husband's job transferred them to California. She then started writing about the Kansas prairie she was homesick for and started her writing career.

Linda's first book, *Butter in the Well*, written as diary entries, is about the Swedish immigrant that homesteaded her family farm. Readers wanted to know what happened to the family, so she continued the story with *Prairie Bloomin'*, *Egg Gravy* (a pioneer cookbook), and *Looking Back.*

Her next historical fiction series features pioneer women as they experience the Civil War firsthand. *Trail of Thread*, *Thimble of Soil*, and *Stitch of Courage*, written in the form of letters, has a quilt theme because of a quilt handed down in Linda Hubalek's family. *Tying the Knot,* in the Kansas Quilter series, continues the storyline through the next generation of Pieratts.

Planting Dreams, Cultivating Hope, and *Harvesting Faith* tells her ancestor's story that changed their family history forever when they homesteaded on the unforgiving Kansas prairie.

Linda Hubalek and her husband eventually moved back home to Kansas, and she continues to write about pioneer women that made Kansas their home.

www.LindaHubalek.com

www.Facebook.com/LindaHubalekbooks

Linda Hubalek's Amazon Page

Order Form- Photocopy or Tear Out Page

Order to: Butterfield Books Inc., PO Box 407, Lindsborg KS 67456

Orders: **1-785-227-9250** Email: **staff@ButterfieldBooks.com**

Order online at www.ButterfieldBooks.com

Send to:

Name ____

Address ____

Town, St ________________________________ Zip ________

☐ **Check** enclosed, payable to **Butterfield Books Inc.**

☐ **Charge my credit card**

____________________________ Exp_____ CVV _____

Signature ______________________________________

Title	Qty	Unit	Total
Butter in the Well		11.95	
Prairie Bloomin'		11.95	
Egg Gravy		11.95	
Looking Back		11.95	
Butter in the Well Series (4 bks)		42.95	
Trail of Thread		11.95	
Thimble of Soil		11.95	
Stitch of Courage		11.95	
Trail of Thread Series (3 bks)		32.95	
Planting Dreams		11.95	
Cultivating Hope		11.95	
Harvesting Faith		11.95	
Planting Dreams Series (3 bks)		32.95	
Tying the Knot		11.95	
Rania Ropes a Rancher		11.95	
		Subtotal	
	KS	add 8.65% tax	
S/H per address: $3.00 for 1st book, Each add'l $.50			
		Total	

Order Form- Photocopy or Tear Out Page

Order to: Butterfield Books Inc., PO Box 407, Lindsborg KS 67456

Orders: **1-785-227-9250** Email: **staff@ButterfieldBooks.com**

Order online at www.ButterfieldBooks.com

Send to:

Name ____

Address ____

Town, St ________________________________ Zip _________

☐ **Check** enclosed, payable to **Butterfield Books Inc.**

☐ **Charge my credit card**

____________________________ Exp_____ CVV _____

Signature ____________________________________

Title	Qty	Unit Price	Total
Butter in the Well		11.95	
Prairie Bloomin'		11.95	
Egg Gravy		11.95	
Looking Back		11.95	
Butter in the Well Series (4 bks)		42.95	
Trail of Thread		11.95	
Thimble of Soil		11.95	
Stitch of Courage		11.95	
Trail of Thread Series (3 bks)		32.95	
Planting Dreams		11.95	
Cultivating Hope		11.95	
Harvesting Faith		11.95	
Planting Dreams Series (3 bks)		32.95	
Tying the Knot		11.95	
Rania Ropes a Rancher		11.95	
		Subtotal	
	KS add	8.65% tax	
S/H per address: $3.00 for 1st book, Each add'l $.50			
		Total	